Capturing the Heart of a Boss 2
Written by Myia White

Dedication

This book is dedicated to the one's whose ever been doubted. Never let nobody tell you what you can and can't do. You hold the power to your limits, let the sky be the limit.

My Readers;

Thank you for rocking with me, with every book that I write you'll always have a piece of me.

Myia White

These Are Our Trying Days - Malia

Sitting in the courtroom with my hands tightly squeezed together as I watched both Zion and the prosecutor go over their arguments made me restless. I tried to sit as still as possible, but seeing Duke up there made me uneasy. His posture was always the same, as he sat up tall and proud. I couldn't see his face and I wish that I could have, I wanted to ease his mind. I knew that he was worried and scared shitless because I was just as scared as he was.

The findings of the prosecutor had the courtroom floored but what I didn't understand was how Zion could have handled his part for Duke? How did they even find out half of the information that they did? Zion is normally always on top of things, so him dropping the ball on this shit was a real convenience. Having to sit and watch them talk about him as if he was a wild animal had me wanting to say something. I watched him sit and listen to them talk about him as if he was a hazard to his environment.

Now understanding his position to a certain degree, I understood why he had to do what he needed to help his family survive. I didn't blame him. I was more scared that his sentencing wasn't going to go in his favor because of this court case.

Hearing the judge automatically throw the case out and placing him in custody until they could give him a new date for sentencing had me giving up all hope. As I watched them put the handcuffs on Duke, I couldn't help but feel like the world came crashing down. Looking at the sadness in his eyes, the weakness in his mother cries and the many voices of the people as they whispered about what had just happened, made the tears that I had been holding in fall faster.

"Jesus, they've got my baby!" his mother cried out as she went up to the podium and tried to hug him.

"Ma'am, you have to get back," the bailiff told her.

"Can I hug him, please?"

He looked at the judge and when he permitted it, his mother hugged him so tight, but he couldn't really hug her back. His sisters saw it and wanted to hug him as well, they formed a family hug and they all cried. I wanted to approach him but it was too late, they had to take him back. Before going to the back, he looked at me and it was as if we spoke without saying a word. He understood my positioning with Zion being in the room and I appreciate him for respecting it. I just wish that I would have taken my ass up there, but now I wouldn't have another chance at seeing him for God knows how long.

His family and I decided to go and have a bite to eat, so we ended up at Ruby Tuesday's. Everyone was so in their feelings and nobody was really saying anything.

"Why the hell are y'all sitting around looking sad? My boy is gone be good, ain't that right, momma?"

"I hope so baby." She looked sadder than before at the mentioning of Duke.

"Hey bro," Lola greeted him as she stood up and gave him a hug.

"Sup y'all?" he mushed Nicole.

"I'm just worried about my baby that's all. Have you met Malia?"

"Malia? The infamous Malia, I mean I've heard of her, but I don't know her."

"Not me; I'm just a small-town city girl."

"I remember you from the kickback a while ago and my boy snatched yo' ass up real quick. He's been hush mouth about you, but I know he fucks with you."

"I know his ass better since I'm his woman."

He fell out of his seat, being all dramatic, which cause everybody at the table to laugh. I was glad that there was a smile upon their faces during this hard time.

"I can't believe it; you finally got my nigga to be tied down. For the longest, I thought that we were gone have to get that fool a cat every year after his 30th birthday."

Lola threw a roll at him. "Don't be talking about my brother like that. He doesn't need no damn cat."

"Watch y'all mouths, I am sitting here." Cathleen looked at the two of them and they both snickered like school kids but they knew better, I could see it.

"Sorry momma, but for real, you know how he shut down after sis," he explained as the table got quiet as if they were trying to spare my feelings. I caught the look between Nicole and Dee; it was like they were speaking code.

"It's okay. He told me about her."

"For real?" Dee asked, covering his mouth.

"Yeah, he did, when we were just getting to know each other."

Everybody looked like he had spilled the ancient Chinese secret or something. The food came and everybody ate in silence with a little bit of conversation. I wouldn't say that it was awkward, but the energy that we normally have wasn't there. I hope that I wasn't making anybody to uncomfortable.

Judgement Day - Duke

"Aye Duke, tomorrow's the day, my nigga," Red told me, he was my cellmate and he was cool but sometimes this nigga didn't know when to shut the fuck up.

They had me here for almost four weeks until they could put me on the calendar. I was nervous about this court date tomorrow and I didn't want a constant reminder of the shit. This could go one of two ways and neither of them will be easy for me, but I got to do what I got do. I got down on the floor to do some sit ups; I needed something to take my mind off me being here and my court case. I did sit-ups until they called out for lunch. I hated eating this nasty shit, but I needed it to survive. I chilled around with a few niggas until they did phone calls that night. I only had ten minutes so I had better use them wisely. I decided to call my momma first. I hadn't really spoken to them in the weeks that I was here. I felt like a failure and it was eating me inside to know that I was inside this jail while they were out there having to fend for themselves.

"Hey pretty lady."

"Hey my baby, I miss you. Are they treating you right?"

"Yeah ma, I'm good, everything's good. I have court tomorrow at 8:30 and I didn't know if my lawyer told you or not."

"You know we'll be there baby"

"Alright pretty lady. I have to call my woman so I'll see y'all tomorrow"

"Okay baby. We are praying for you and we love you Zay."

"Love you too." As soon as I hung up, I dialed Malia's number and waited to hear her voice.

"Baby!" I could feel her smile through the phone as it gave me a little glimmer of hope. We talked for the last few minutes and I informed her of my court date tomorrow, she informed me that she would be there and we ended the call.

After our calls it was light outs, not to long after and then it hit me that tomorrow was my judgement day. I didn't know if I should be happy or scared, but I think that I was content because I know that I'm not walking out of that courtroom tomorrow. I've accepted my fate; I just pray that the Lord have mercy on my soul.

***

"All rise," the bailiff announced as Judge Banes came in.

The pit of nervousness in my stomach had me wanting to throw up. It was finally time for my sentencing after I had been in Fulton County Jail knowing that prison awaits me. I looked behind me and saw my mother, sisters, Dee and of course Malia. They all looked so beautiful but scared as can be. I nodded my head at them as we waited for the judge to sit down. I knew that this was do or die right now. In my mind, it wasn't looking too good for me.

My case began and those minutes felt like hours as I watched Zion beg for my freedom. There was so much I wanted to say to plead my own case, but what was there to say? I keep fucking up but I promise that I won't do it again? Naw, these people weren't trying to hear that from a convicted felon, they wanted to see their tax dollars be put to great use and getting me off the streets will satisfy their urge until another nigga can be put away. Although they didn't know my story, that won't matter; all they see is a nigga with tattoos everywhere and instantly judgment happens.

"Your Honor, my client has been on his best behavior while being detained. I ask the courts to see that he's trying and give him a chance?" Zion asked the courts after his opening statement. Then the prosecutor Sandra came up and I knew that she was getting ready to send me to hell on a way one street.

"Zayvier Butler is a convicted felon who has violated the state laws and has violated the last chance that we gave him before. Clearly, he hasn't learned his lesson. He was in an altercation while knowing that he was on thin ice."

I watched her walk away. Hearing her talk about me like I was a third grade child, made me want to curse her ass out. The rest of my case was like classmate vs. classmate wanting the title of winning. All that was on my mind was my family and building my relationship with Malia. I know that this arrest has put a wall up within our relationship. I can't be mad if we aren't the same after this.

We came back from recess and the feeling that I had didn't sit well with me. I swear if I didn't have these shackles on my feet and handcuffs on my hands, I would try to run but that meant six bullets to the back for me. I made this mess and now I must deal with the consequences. Everything up until the verdict was a blur.

"Guilty," the jurors said and I heard whispers amongst the people in the courtroom. I heard my mother as she began to cry and I wanted to run and hug her.

"Mr. Zayvier Butler, you were in violation of your probation. For that, I sentence you to the maximum of two years. For your drug charges, I sentence you to three years both consecutive." He banged his gavel and the scream that came from my mother crushed my soul more than hearing the verdict.

I wouldn't be able to walk the streets for five fucking years. I now had limited phone calls and visitation, not to mention somebody telling me when to eat and wash my ass for five got damn years. This was a hard pill to swallow, but it's my life for the next five years. I prayed that my nigga Dee held me down on the outside like I knew that he would. I knew that I wasn't walking out of the courtroom a free man. Hearing the judge give me five years made my knees weak. I wanted to shed a few tears for the disappointment that I placed upon my family but mainly myself. I had been trying to get my shit straight and I ended back up in jail. The look on my families faces when I had to give them a hug for the last time crushed me. I wanted to apologize to them for several reasons. The frog in my throat wouldn't allow me to speak my last words to them. I just wanted to savor the last moments. Looking at Malia as her eyes filled with tears and hurt, I wanted her more than anything. She held her body while she shared a stare or two with me. She began to walk up towards the podium but I was being taken back. I wasn't mad that I couldn't hug her goodbye because I know that this was a lot for her. I found her looking at Zion a few times as a warning to me, so I knew that she was trying to stay low.

I had to wait downstairs to get on the van to go to the prison. They still had people doing trials and they needed to get on the van as well. On the ride to the prison, everybody was trying to get to know each other. I didn't want to be bothered, I just wanted peace and quiet. Going through the whole booking process and being giving everything that I would need while being here, it seemed like I was taking that mile walk of death as I was being escorted to my cell. Once I entered the cell and the doors closed behind me, I knew that this was my reality. There was nobody in the bunk with me and I was grateful because I didn't want to be bothered with anybody. I undressed and dressed in my jumpsuit and climbed on the bunk. Staring in the dark as a little light peered through the cell, began to feel the hurt and pain as I let my thoughts take over me.

I saw my momma and sisters face flash across with their beautiful smiles; I went through an array of family moments. Seeing their smiles and hearing their laughter, I began to smile. It played like a motion picture movie in my mind and I enjoyed front row seat. I laughed at this incident that happened when between my sisters and I played *Jerry Springer* in the living room and I was the host and both Nicole and Lola was my guests playing like they were dating the same nigga. It started out real cool until words were said that shouldn't have been and they began fighting. Nicole threw Lola's ass into the closet door and broke it off the hinge. They were really in that bitch thumping; it was funny to me. I tried to break them up but I couldn't, they were really going at it. My mother came in, broke it up, and beat the hell out of all of us. Lola's arm was broken and until it healed, my mother beat our ass every time she thought about it.

My mind switched from them to Malia. In this short amount of time, I've grown very fond of her. To be honest, she makes a nigga feel like everything will be alright. Everything about her was what I needed in my life, she complimented what I was trying to do with the vision I had in life. I saw her going through the most detrimental event of her life and she bounced back ten toes up. Remembering the very first time that I saw her and remembering the look of unsureness in her eyes. She was putting up one hell of a front for that husband of hers, knowing that their marriage was damned near over. I've seen a few faces of hers and I loved the way that she can transform from being dressed classy to jeans and sneakers and had no problem doing it. I hated the way that fool had stripped her of her self-confidence and I'm mad that she didn't see the ability to be above just being a little housewife. She was so much more than she gave herself credit for; she was perfect in my eyes, even through the flaws. I appreciate the flaws because I'm flawed as well, what we were building ways turning into something beautiful. I was having to play it all the way cool, because I wasn't about to be labeled as a bitch nigga.

Many thoughts of my life and family made a nigga heart grow weak. My eyes started to get dry or at least that's what I told myself as my face moved across this tear stained my pillow. Damn! I really fucked up. I wanted to close my eyes for sleep after staring off into space for what seemed like an eternity, but I couldn't, I had nervous energy. Staring into the dark some more I heard my heart beating through my chest, I had to cope with my reality as I dozed off to sleep the best way that I could.

I Won't Let You Go - Zion

After a long ass day, I was finally ready to get home and chill with my baby girl. I wanted some Chinese food, so I went and picked up some before going home. I pulled up to the house and my mom's car was here. I wasn't for her bullshit today, ever since she confessed how she really felt about her relationship with my father; she's been hiding between my home and hers. I couldn't complain because she was babysitting without a fee so I could save some money.

"Hello Zion, dear," she greeted as Mariah cooed in her arms for me. I placed the food on the counter and picked her up.

"What's going on, ma?"

"Nothing much. How was your day?" She busied around the kitchen, fixing food.

"Long but expected."

She walked over to the bag and looked inside. The roll of her eyes and the deep sigh was letting me know that I was in for a lecture that I really didn't want to hear. I walked to the refrigerator, grabbed me a Guinness beer and sat back in my spot because I was ready to eat.

"I need to talk to you."

"Go ahead, ma." I placed Mariah in her bouncer and sat down at the table.

"I hate the mess that you've made of your life. You lost a great woman and now you have a child that you barely know what to do with."

She would be the one to talk; she was a wife to a nigga who stayed fucking around. Now she wants to preach to the choir like her shit was just straight. I let her have her moment because I didn't want to have this argument with her. I was feeling great, I was one step closer to getting my life back and she wasn't about to fuck up my mood. Malia wasn't gone she was just still pissed at me; she'll be back.

"I know, ma. I'll get it right, but let's sit and eat before I go to bed. I'm tired and I just want peace tonight," I pleaded with her. She took the bait and we ate in silence.

After we were done eating, she left and she took Mariah with her because I had an early day tomorrow and I didn't want the hassle of calling over the nanny when her ass was doing absolutely nothing and she could just watch her instead of me paying someone else.

After I was out of the shower, my phone rung and it was Tamela. She had asked me earlier could she come by, at first I was against it and then I thought about it. It had been a minute since I got my dick wet so I told her to come over. I waited for her and ended up dozing off; the doorbell and my phone ringing at the same time awakened me. I wiped the drool from my face and splash water on it before going to answer the door.

"I thought you were reneging on your offer," Tamela greeted with a trench coat on and bottle of Rose' in her hands.

I didn't even have to move to the side as she let herself in the house. I got a good look at that ass swinging underneath that trench and I knew it was going to be a good night. Damn work, I would have to think about that later; being tired at the office was well worth it. She walked upstairs and I let her, I was too hypnotized by what was under the coat to stop her.

"Last room on the left."

I just followed her upstairs. She was dropping clothing items as she led up the stairs, the first being the trench coat. She had on nothing but some red fuck-me pumps and the calves on her extended legs had me ready to climb that tree. Entering the room, I wasted no time and kissed the purple lipstick that was painted perfectly on her lips off. She smelled like peaches or something and I now had a very intense sweet tooth. I walked her over to the bed and laid her down.

"That's how you feel, baby?" I placed my mouth on hers and sucked on her tongue.

"Yes, and I'm ready to show you how I feel." Pushing her back on the bed, she was spread eagle. I saw the lust that she had in her eyes for me and I matched the very same look. I knew that she wanted me to make love to her body, but all I wanted was a quick fuck.

I needed a way to get my wife back. I didn't want to hear anything coming from Malia other than "*yes, I'll take you back*" or

"I forgive you baby". I invested too many years into that bitch for her to up and think that she was going to leave me. I let her leave because she wanted to spread her wings, but she took it too far when she decided to ride that nigga's dick.

I was going to get her back if it was the last thing that I did. I was tired of playing her little game. I get it, I fucked up but she can come home now. That nigga couldn't do anything for her behind bars and I made sure of it. A woman like Malia needs lots attention and affection; that nigga don't look as if he can please her in any way, not like me.

"Shit baby," Tamela moaned.

I forgot that I was even fucking her; I looked at her through squinted eyes because this wasn't her face, body, or voice— it was Malia. I looked at her thick body hungrily, I missed this moment; I longed for this moment for months. My baby has returned home; I missed her so much. Looking at the last of the purple lipstick on her beautiful full lips, I had to kiss her. Staring at the beautiful face of hers, I wanted to taste her tongue so I hungrily kissed her. I missed this face, this was a face that I had seen for ten years.

I fucked her the way that I knew she loved to be fucked. I wrapped my hands around her throat and I beat that pussy out of commission, or at least tried. I wanted to hit the bottom of her stomach. If I could, I'll put in her chest. Malia's pussy had me right at home.

"Baby, you're hurting me!" she squealed, trying to catch her breath.

"Shhhh… baby… just enjoy it." I kissed on her neck, enjoying her sweet-smelling skin. I was about to give her what she's been missing.

"Just like that," she moaned, becoming a pawn in my game. She knew that she couldn't resist her husband, I taught her how to fuck so I knew what she was capable of. Listening to the gushiness of her wet ass pussy, I smiled because it still sounded the same.

"I missed you," I recited, looking into her eyes as I've done plenty of days for ten years. There was a glimmer in them and it looked like she was on the verge of tears. I was going to fuck her to make her remember that I'm king. I wanted this pussy to hurt. Pumping vigorously, I spelled my name in her vaginal walls.

I heard a scream, her body was shaking and that's what I wanted. I wanted to feel that warm liquid coat my dick like it used to.

"Give daddy that sweet shit," I grunted, pressing her legs into the bed. My climax was on the edge and I needed her position just right to get what I wanted. I positioned her and it was all walls. She cooed, moaned, and rubbed on me, which did it for me. "I'm cumming baby," I moaned out like a bitch, but I didn't care, I needed her to know what she was doing to me.

"Cum baby!"

"Maallllliiiaaa…" I screamed out as I filled her up with my kids. My knees were weak, my legs were shaking, and my abs was contracting. Wiping the sweat from my eyes; finally opening them.

"Did you call me Malia?" I looked at whom I remember as Tamela. I couldn't even lie to her, so I got off the bed and went to take a shower. I almost felt bad when I looked at her and saw the disappointment in her eyes.

"I'm talking to you, Zion. Is my pussy that whack that you had to call me your ex's name?" She stood in the bathroom doorway, chastising me.

I wanted to tell her that her pussy didn't compare, but I was short on my women so I had to keep her around. She had some good head, it wasn't like Angela's or Malia's, but she'll do until I taught her everything that she needs to know on pleasing me.

"Look, I apologize for that shit." I got into the shower, closing the door. If she wanted to join me then she had better let that shit go and come and take a shower. I didn't owe anyone an explanation of why I do the shit that I do. First, it was Malia, then Angela and now Tamela the women in my life just didn't know their place. She knew that I loved Malia and she wasn't going to change that.

Secrets of the envelope - Malia

I needed to channel my energy. I was all over the place and my house wasn't getting it for me today. I've lounged around pretty much all morning and there was something missing. It was my day off and I decided to clean up around Duke's home because I couldn't sleep. Plenty of days I went from his home to mine. I just wanted him to come home, but I knew that it wasn't going to happen, at least not anytime soon. Being in his home gave me some peace and understanding of his being away. I had my music playing and got to work. His house wasn't dirty, but it wasn't as tidy as it normally is. The day that he was sentenced I stayed at my own home, but I'd come by at night just to go to sleep in his bed, because I was missing him. The feelings that I have for him are unexplainable and I would rather leave them as is, until I can figure out what's happening to me.

I started in his kitchen and didn't realize just how big his kitchen was, until I began wiping the stainless steel down, scrubbing floor, and cleaning out the refrigerator. My music had me in the mood. Next on my list was his living room and I decided to clean out his big ass fish tank. I was scared because there was a baby shark in there, but that thing was just lazy.

Russ's "Losin' Control" blared through his surround sound. Listening to the shaking of the speakers, I just knew that I was going to be picking up glass from the floor.

"She's fallin' in love now/ Losin' control now/ Fightin' the truth/ Tryin' to hide"

I sang my heart out because this song expressed how I felt about Duke, but I couldn't find my own words. I wouldn't call it love but I would say that now that I have him in my life, I didn't want to let him leave. Through our short time, I've never felt so alive. Regardless of his position right now, I was still happy, happier than I was with someone that I gave ten years of my life to. His face kept replaying in my mind, what has this man done to me? I don't want to fall head over heels just to be shitted on again or worse, what if he doesn't feel the same? I would have to think about that later. I was going to enjoy the high of this stimulating relationship.

I began dusting his fireplace, not really being able to reach it the way that I wanted. Wiping his pictures, I smiled at his handsome face. Looking at the many pictures of him and his family, who were was his world that was a beautiful thing. Mistakenly hitting a picture and it fell on the ground. I began picking up the pieces that I could. There was a key in the pile of glass; not thinking too much of it, I placed the key inside of my pocket while I cleaned up the mess. After cleaning up downstairs, I went upstairs, cleaning the most used rooms and bathrooms. Going into his room, I placed clothes into the hampers so I could start washing them. His closet was the messiest; things were everywhere. I straightened it out to the best of my ability. As I was straightening up in clothes on the rack there was a yellow envelope that caught my eye.

What is this? I thought to myself. Moving on to the next rack, I couldn't help looking at over my shoulder at the envelope.

"No Malia, you won't snoop. Build trust," I recited to myself.

Nevertheless, it kept my attention and I needed to see what it was. Picking it up, it was a black kiss on the envelope. Now my radar went off and I wanted to open it. I hope that he wasn't fucking around on me. I didn't want to think about it, but there was a possibility for anything. Placing it back where I found it, I finished straightening up and went into his bathroom. Turning up the music, I scrubbed and cleaned.

"That shit will continue to bother you. Just do it, you'll find out the truth. Either he's fucking with you or not," I chanted.

Placing the cleaning cloth on the sink, I marched back into his closet and went for the envelope again. I took a deep breath before opening it.

Dear Honey Buns;

I just want you to know that I love you, but I have my secrets and I'm afraid that when it's all over that you'll hate me. I want nothing more than to make you happy; I just have to figure out how. I've done some things that you may or may not forgive me about. When I first entered the deal, it was only supposed to be business, but then I got to know the real Zayvier and overtime I fell in love with you. You are truly a remarkable man; you just don't know it. The way that you love is truly amazing and I've felt nothing more than your love since the day that we discovered our love. I hate myself for not being honest about some things, but now that doesn't matter and our time is limited. My time is limited and there isn't much that I can do. I'm sorry about everything, I'm sorry that I lied and I'm sorry for the hurt that you're going to experience. However, most of all I'm sorry that you won't get to meet your child. I have to go now, but just know that I'll always love you, even in death.

Your baby lumps

Instant jealousy filled my bones as I read this letter, as this woman express her feelings for my man. Not understanding what all the other shit that she was saying in this letter meant, all I saw was love one too many times. Looking over the letter once more, I saw that she was pregnant with his child. He has a baby and hasn't even thought of mentioning it. Where was his baby mother now? I know he wasn't keeping her and his child a secret.

"What the kind of person are you Duke?" I asked aloud. I had to remind myself that I was snooping and I shouldn't be mad, but I wasn't about to feel played and I wasn't going to allow him to hurt me. I pondering over the letter for a bit, until I decided to put it back. I felt myself getting pissed and antsy, I couldn't ask him because I haven't talked to him in weeks. For the most part, I was done cleaning. I had a few loads of clothes to do, so I took them and decided to wash them at my house, the longer that I was here, the more that I would allow that letter to plague my mind. I couldn't help myself as I grabbed the clothes; I had to go back for the letter.

After loading the clothes into the car, I called Sasha.

"Boo, what are you doing?"

"Nothing, just relaxing. What's up, you good?"

"I need to talk to you. Can I come over?"

"I'll be here. Are you sure you're alright?"

I told her that I was fine as I locked up Duke's home and left to go to her house. I placed the envelop on the seat and the whole time I drove, it was like the letter was taunting me. Why couldn't I think straight? I stopped by the convenience store for a Coke to calm my nerves because I was that on edge. If I sat still long enough, my nerves would work themselves into overload. Sasha's house was almost twenty minutes away from his house and I swear that it felt like I was never going to get there.

"Ugh!" I yelled annoyed as hell. There was traffic and any and everything was getting on my nerves.

I think the fact that I haven't spoken to him in weeks made this more difficult for me. I finally pulled up to her house and I felt a sense of relief. She opened the door the moment that she saw my car pull up. I grabbed the envelope and walked past her and into the house.

"Well, hello to you to Malia," she spoke with attitude.

I had to collect myself when I saw her. This wasn't her issue, but I was confused and I think I was mad. I wasn't sure if I was mad for the right reasons, which is why I was coming to her so that she could help me figure it out.

"I'm sorry. I need your understanding and your clearer head sis." I wiped the beads of sweat from my forehead. It was still cold outside, so why was I sweating? I placed the letter on her coffee table and took a seat.

"What's this?" she asked looking at me and eyeing the letter suspiciously.

"A letter that I found at Duke's house while I was cleaning."

"Mal—"

"I wasn't snooping Sasha, I promise. I was honestly cleaning and I found this while I was cleaning his closet."

She opened the letter and I watched her the whole time while she read over the letter; her eyes had gotten big a few times too. I wondered what she was thinking. When she finished, I couldn't understand her expression anymore. It was like she wanted to be on the fence about it.

"Well, whoever this girl is loves him. However, at the same time, she has some secrets that she doesn't want him to know but at the same time, she does want him to know. The fact that she's pregnant blew me. Where is she? Who is she? There is a nickname here but that's it." She picked up the letter again, trying to get a clearer understanding.

"I don't know but I felt someway reading. Like another female is madly in love with my man and from the looks of it, he loves her ass too. Sasha, what the hell kind of games is she playing?" I yelled because now that I think about it, I went against my marriage vows for him.

Although my husband had already gone against our vows, I still felt bad for even thinking about Duke. He chased me, not the other way around, and the whole time he had whole fucking family. I didn't ask to be here and then to be shitted on too, no fucking way! I asked him to keep it 8 more than 92 with me and he lied. I hope that I'm overacting.

"Calm down boo," she consoled me with pats on the back and a bottle of water. She knew that I was in overload and was about to have an anxiety attack. I couldn't stop the thoughts from racing and it was too much. I wasn't about to be another fool.

"I'm trying but what would you do? What do I do?"

"First, you calm down with your crazy ass. Then, we think about this and be rational. There is a logical explanation for this. I've only met Duke once or twice, but I can pick up on vibes and you know that. Nothing about him seems like he would be fucking around on you. Not to this extent, so what I need you to do is relax. You opened his mail, that's mistake one. Now you're in your feelings. You know the saying don't go looking because you just may find something. I'm not saying that you went looking, but you didn't have to open that letter. It's hidden for a reason. Clearly, he hasn't read it yet. That letter is deep as fuck and there is no telling what that girl meant by anything that she said; all we know is that she loved him and she's pregnant."

She made sense; I'm still in my feelings, but I must be rational about this. I just couldn't take being made a fool of again, especially when I didn't ask for any of this. I fell for the trap and now I'm out here probably looking all types of crazy. Then again, I've got to try and talk to Duke about this. Yet, how do I bring up that I invaded his space? We talked about the situation a little bit more and I was able to calm down. I had my moment but I had to really think about it. I was going to take the letter back to his house and almost forget the situation, knowing it wasn't going to be easy. I have to try because I can't treat him bad because of someone else's mistakes. I was on edge and although I calmed down, this will bother me. I hoped for his sake that it better had been an old letter. I stayed with her for a little while longer before I decided to get home before it got to dark outside and I had to take these loads of clothes up the stairs to my home.

The whole ride home, I was on edge. Now that I wasn't around Sasha, my thoughts were back at square one, just not as bad. I listened to the radio and enjoyed the music to clear my mind to the best of its ability. I thought about Duke and I wished that the answers would jump out me before I made a fool of myself. Looking in my mirror, there was a dark figure in the car behind me. They were on my bumper so closely, that if I stopped on brakes they would come through my car. I sped up because I didn't have time for this and they sped up as well. Thankfully, my exit was next; they tailed me all the way until I got off the highway.

These Niggas Want To Test Me – Duke

I was on four number three in this hellhole. This was a reality check for me. I haven't made any calls or wrote anyone; I'm still wrapping my head around this shit. The words of the judge are the only thing that I keep hearing and my mother's screams are the ones that I keep feeling. Malia's tears are the very ones that stained my pillows, when I was in the mood to shed a few. I don't know if I could handle people telling me when it was time for me to get up and go to sleep. I had to adjust, showering with hell of niggas, no real meals, no real outside communication, not being able to be who I want to be and just being around hard legs all the time. We had to do things per others and I hated it. I came in quietly observing my surroundings and I saw a few niggas that I knew from around the way. I had a few that wanted to say something to me by making conversation and try to get cool with me, but I wasn't on that right now. My mindset was on serving this time and not making friends.

As we sat in the cafeteria, I picked over my food. I didn't care for it too much; it was slop. I was going to have money placed on my books soon after I got settled in the way that I wanted to. I sat by myself because I was being observant. Giving a few head nods to the people that gave me one as they passed, I focused on the bullshit of a meal in front of me. Some stale ass meatloaf, weak mash potatoes that was white inside of a hint of color from the butter, and some hard ass corn that wasn't cooked all the way. I went for the nasty ass cornbread instead and drank my milk. We had another ten minutes left and I was ready to leave so that I could go to the television room, which was the only thing that I could look forward to right now.

Being the first one in the television room, I made myself comfortable and turned the television to some boring ass movie. The channel selection on the television was limited. Kicking my feet up and chilling, I enjoyed what I could. It wasn't long before everyone came in and disturbed my peace. Never saying a word, I tried my best to enjoy the movie.

"Don't nobody want to watch this shit!" somebody yelled from behind me. I stayed looking straight ahead, paying them no mind. Many people agreed with him, igging the situation on further than it needed to be. I was just hoping and praying that they let the shit go and move around. No pussy was in my blood and if they wanted to be down with the shits then we could move some furniture. I listened to them talk behind me but nobody ever addressed me.

"I'll get that up outchea." Some dude came and snatched the remote from my hands. I jumped up so fast because he was in my personal space and he put his hands on me.

"Nigga, have you lost your mothafuckin' mind?" I sneered as our noses touch, from being so close. His boys were still igging him on.

"I said nobody wanted to watch that bullshit." He laughed.

"I don't give a fuck what y'all niggas wanna do, but you violated pussy, when you came up in my personal space."

"Oooooo… You gone let that nigga talk to you like that?" they asked him.

I saw the way that his chest was heaving so I knew that we were gone get ready to lock up. I smirked at him because I already knew what was about to be happen. Never being the one to let people see me sweat; the only one that gets to see that is my lady, when I'm blowing her back out. He pushed me hard as hell and that sent me stumbling backwards. I had to catch my balance because he was coming towards me at a fast speed. He was an inch or so taller than me, so this shit was about to be a match. As soon as he came towards me, I threw three quick ones that he wasn't able to catch. I watched his head go from side to side as it started leaking. He tried to catch himself and I tackled him on the ground. Sending more powerful blows, I was sent flying off of him. He had a tray in his hand that cracked on my head when he hit me with it. Shaking it off before he tried to get on top of me, I uppercut him and he flew off me. I had no time to think since he was struggling to get up. I came down on him with a chair, repeatedly. I blacked out from throwing this chair at his ass and the next thing I remembered is being escorted to the infraction and people picking dude's unconscious body off the ground. It took me a minute before I was taken to the hole.

"Fuck!" I yelled as I threw a punch to the brick wall. How the fuck did I let a nigga knock me off like that? I was too pissed to even realize that I was confined to this box for twenty-three hours with one hour of sunlight maybe. I sat in this box thinking about some shit, some evil shit because I hadn't come down off my trip. I looked at the wall and I had to get my mind right. I ended up falling asleep and was awakened by the guard.

"Get the fuck up." He kicked my cot. This just wasn't my day. These niggas wanted to test me and I was going to fail miserably. I kept my back turned as I adjusted my eyes, turning over slowly.

"So, you're the big shit that beat Moe's ass, huh?" He smirked.

I didn't have time for this shit, man. He knew the answer to the question, that's why he came into my room off muscle. I sat up and adjusted my shirt. I got myself together and just sat there looking at his ass. He had to be a buck eighty-five soak and wet; he wasn't a match for me. I wasn't about to let him run up on me on no bullshit and if I had to go out, it was going to be with a fight. His presence was annoying the fuck out of me.

"What do you want, man?"

He walked out of the room and came back with my dinner. He must be a fool if he thought that I was a fool to take food from him or anybody else up in this bitch.

"I came to give the champ his meal." He smirks, dropping my plate of food on the floor.

I laughed as I ran my hand down my face, looking at the bullshit of food on the floor. I had to think logically because they wanted this from me.

"You ain't gone eat?" He laughed, trying to be funny. I wasn't moved, I was insulted and it was only so much of his bullshit that I was going to take.

"I'll eat it right after you, fuck boy.'" I laughed to get under his skin.

"Fuck boy?" He looked around the room like there was somebody here. I looked with him because maybe there was and I just couldn't see their ass.

"You treating me like a fucking animal and any nigga fucking with a nigga while he's out is a fuck boy!" I spat with so much venom he was going to feel the cuts of my words. I'm not like these other niggas; I am a one man army.

"You might want to talk to me nice because I can make your life a living hell. I ain't no inmate."

I don't know if he thought he was putting fear in my heart. I could give two fucks about what he was saying; he wasn't about to try me— inmate, warden, guard or whatever. I was going to hold my own.

"I don't give a fuck who you are." I looked at the food on the floor and watched him, while I kicked the tray back outside.

"It's just day one nigga; you have some ways to go." He laughed, while he closed the door to my cell and left me there. There I was again looking at the wall and an even more pissed off attitude. These niggas really wanted to see me. I guess it's time.

When I came from the hole, I made sure to make my rounds so that these niggas knew who I was. But, somebody beat me to the punch. My name is floating through the prison so fast that I didn't have time to accept or deny anything. Putting money in people's pockets around here to make some things happen. Having a few on payroll, I was going to make sure that I had what I needed as long as I was here. I couldn't wait to see my family and my woman.

When You Touch Me, You Do It To Me Every Time - Malia

After finding the letter almost two weeks ago, I still hadn't brought it up. I haven't even spoken to him, which make this so much worse than what it was. I wasn't as mad as before because I had to do some thinking on it for a while. I was letting my thoughts get the best of me. I was going to bring it up today, needing to get to the bottom of it.

I looked over my outfit and made sure that I looked perfect. If he told me anything other than the truth and I picked up on it, I was giving him a mental to remember me by. I wasn't about to play these games with him. I would hate to have to end our relationship, but I have to do what's best for me.

Today was the first time that I could visit him. He says that it's because he wanted to get settled in first and see how things operated. I knew it's because he didn't want me to see him in there like that. I didn't see him any differently than before he went in. I knew his situation before we got involved and that was still my decision to deal with him after it all.

"You're ready boo," Lo asked as she entered Duke's master bedroom where I had been staying instead of my own home. I felt that staying here, kept me close to him. I slept in his shirts every night and held his pillow close. I felt his presence when I was here; it kept me at peace most days.

I did a once over, I fixed my sew-in into a sloppy ponytail and I was ready. Lo and I were the first to go and visit him because his mother said that she couldn't take seeing her baby like that. His sister, Nicole had to handle some business so she would go next time. We headed down the road; it would take us at least an hour to get to him.

"You okay, Lo?" She had been distant lately, almost as if she was avoiding something.

"I'm fine honey. Why do you ask that?"

"You aren't yourself lately. Talk to me."

She explained that she was in a relationship and that she and her boyfriend decided to part ways. Needing time to herself, especially with everything going on, she's deciding to give herself some space. I had to respect that because I was once in that mental space when I broke up with Zion.

"How are you on the other hand?" She dropped the conversation about her.

"I'm good as can be," I lied because some days I wanted to cry more than a little bit.

"I know you are. I can see the physical, but what about the mental?"

I let out a sigh. "Lo, some days I feel sadder than others. But, I have to be strong because I knew what was to come."

"You know, as much as Zayvier tried to be strong, I knew he feared the outcome. Somewhere in my heart, I knew that he knew that he wasn't going to walk out of the court room one day."

"I knew that he knew it as well. I applaud him for handling the situation like he did. He made sure that everyone was taken care of and everything was in order."

Duke had left me well over a million dollars. The day that he was sentenced I received a notification from my bank about a deposit. I had a decent amount of money because I had started working for a new law firm. So I thought maybe that my paycheck had hit my account, when I opened it, there it was in black that my available balance was $1,003,630. I thought that the bank made a mistake and I called to check it. They ensured me that everything was legit. I didn't think anything of it, until Lola and I talked awhile later and Duke had told her that he placed it in there and to look out for me. I was grateful for what he did, but I couldn't accept that and to let a man take care of me. After giving it much thought, I removed what he placed in my account and hid it out of sight and out of mind.

The moment that we pulled up to the prison, my stomach started doing backflips. This would be the first time that I saw him since he was sentenced almost a month ago. I looked at Lola, as she wiped the tears from her eyes and patted her back.

"I'm fine boo. Let's go and see this big headed fool." She laughed but I can tell that she wanted to cry.

Playing along with her I got out of the car. The smell of the jailhouse made me nauseous and nervous. I looked around at the many families, many women that held newborns and had children running around while trying to keep calm. I felt bad for a few because while they held newborns they had one or two children running around the waiting room. They looked so defeated and on top of that, the father of their kids was behind these very bars. I picked up an old magazine and flip through the pages to distract me while we waited.

We were finally allowed to go back after we damn near emptied our whole identities into a locker. I walked behind Lola as we entered the visitor's room. Looking around the room, we all took seats at the tables. There wasn't an inmate in sight, but after a few minutes' inmates were pouring into the room. I watched inmate after inmate come in and find their families, hearing the cries that came from some women, the words "daddy" being screamed by a few kids, and witness the ray of emotions in the room. I impatiently waited as all the inmates had come into the room. However, not all, because Duke wasn't here.

"Where the hell is Zayvier Butler?" Lola stood up and asked the guard. The big black guard stood there with his hand on his belt looking unfazed about her being that close to him.

With a chuckle he replied, "Ma'am, calm down and backup." He looked down on her.

"No, you go back there and bring out inmate 12874759-0 now!"

"Come with me." Another guard pointed to her. That "come with me" calmed all that hostility bullshit that she was on as she looked at me and backed up. Standing up next to her, I wasn't about to let them try to lock her up for no good reason, nor did I plan on missing and not seeing Duke either; so we were going to have to come to some type of agreement for the time being.

"Are you Lola and Malia?" he asked us. Looking at each other trying to figure out how he knew our names as we stood still. "Come with me." He walked off and I shrugged my shoulders and grabbed her hand as we followed him. It seemed as if we were on the mile walk before we finally made it to wherever we were. We were on the outside of the prison. I looked around in confusion. I hope she didn't just get us kicked out.

"Why did you bring us out here?" I turned around and asked him as he stood in the doorway. The guard just looked at me like I wasn't asking him a question. I was fussing at him and Lola was as well.

"Yo' ass is impatient as hell. I tell you the truth." I turned around as I heard Duke's voice behind me. I stood there for a while and took in his appearance. Nothing much has changed, but he was getting a little bigger with muscle. "So you just gone stand there staring at a nigga?" He began walking up to me. I took off running to him and he caught me midway, kissing him on contact.

"Hey baby, I thought that I wasn't going to get to see you." I kissed his juicy lips some more.

"Never that baby. I haven't seen yo' thick ass in almost two and a half months and haven't touched you in three, this visit was a must. Three and a half months' total without being close to you, girl." We hugged a little bit longer and shared a few more lasting kisses. The feel of his broad shoulders, strong arms and his warmth made me feel at ease. I missed this beautiful ass man.

"Ummm… I am standing here," Lola finally spoke up.

"My bad sis. I had to show my baby some love." He looked over my shoulder at her. I tapped him so that he could place me on the ground.

"I know but damn you act like I wasn't here. If I hadn't said anything. I just knew that y'all were gone be fucking on the ground." She laughed as she walked up to him and he hugged the both of us.

I moved out of the hug so that they could have their moment. I looked at the two of them and the bond that they shared was so special. She held onto him for dear life and I could tell that she was crying because of the movement that she was doing. They let go and my suspicions were confirmed as she wiped her eyes. We walked to the table nearby and took a seat.

"How you been, baby?" he asked me as he caressed the back of my hand as I sat next to him and Lola sat on the other side of the table.

"I've been good baby, just working trying to get my money up and taking care of home. How have you been?"

"I put money in your account. What did you do with it, Malia?" he asked in a serious tone.

"I tried to figure out where that money came from for the longest and then it occurred to me that you must've gotten it in there somehow. I took it and I hid it until you come home. That's not my money and I don't want a man feeling like he must take care of me. I had enough of that with Zion and I won't have you doing it too. I'm capable of taking care of myself, baby. Thank you for the offer baby, but no thank you."

"Lo, give us a minute."

I looked at Lola as she got up and moved away from the table walking and back into the building. She didn't look mad, but she looked at me like I made a mistake. She was being extra by leaving us altogether, all she had to do was walked off for a second. He turned around with his legs gapped and I was in the center of them.

"Why did you send her away? I said what I had to say."

"I know what you did now you gone listen to me. I'm in this fucking cage and I can't provide for the woman that I adore. I had you taken care of because as long as I'm alive and my heart beats with this blood, I will always and forever take care of you. That nigga really fucked up your mind baby; I'm not here to hurt you. I already let you down when I ended up in this hellhole. I knew I shouldn't have dragged you in a relationship with me knowing that there was a greater possibility of being out in here. I did my dirt and even though I can't see you physically every day, I will forever have your back if you have my front. You hear me, Malia?"

I shook my head like a girl who just got told off by her parents and didn't have the right words; guess he told my ass off. Looking into those big brown eyes, I got stuck in a trance similar to the one when I met him. I bit my bottom lip and he smirked at me.

"You want that, huh?" he cockily asked as he placed a kiss on my neck and pulled me into him. I shivered. "I've been wanting you since that day that I saw you at the bar. Even when I had the pussy, I wanted the pussy; I crave the pussy because that pussy was made for me." He ran his tongue across my ear, placing a kiss on it. The sounds of his kiss sent my body in flames, as I turned my face to him. Hungrily taking his mouth to mine, I tried to kiss the spearmint out of it.

"You want it?" he asked again and nothing registered to me when I answered.

"I need it, baby."

"Are you my rider or what?" He smirked and at that moment, I knew that I fucked up. I wanted him and I wanted him bad, it's been a minute.

"Till the wheels fall off." He didn't respond as he kissed me again. I turned around in the seat as I let his hands roam my body. I couldn't think about what was about to happen as he set my soul on fire. Pulling me forward as he stood up, never breaking the kiss. Picking up and laying me on the table.

"Wait, what's happening?" I asked, but he silenced me with his look.

He began pulling down my pants. Placing kisses on the inside of my moist upper thighs, licking me just right. I looked up at sky as Duke licked and sucked in my pussy like a slushy. The feeling that ran through my body was indescribable, I wanted to scream but my words and screams were stuck in my throat.

"I missed the way that this pussy taste, gurl." He ran a circle over my clit that sent a chill so deep down my spine that I felt myself jump out of my skin.

"Ye...yesss baby!" I moaned as I rotated my hips. I squeezed my eyes tightly as he licked me to his beat. The thoughts of missing his tongue made my body call out to him.

"I've dreamt of this moment since I've been in here." He sucked on my clit so nicely as he spoke; the vibrations from his voice became in sync with him. My body obeyed his every command without him having to say a word.

"I'm cumming, what the fuckkkk?" I screamed out. As my body began to violently shake, I placed my hands over my eyes because I didn't want those near to hear me. I wasn't embarrassed, but I wanted to be able to come back and see my man. I didn't think I could have
come any faster; my body responded in a timely manner. I felt his hands leave my thighs and then I felt him perfectly filling me up.

"Ahhh, I see you been a good girl for daddy," he moaned as I had finally opened my eyes and to see him staring at me. I bite my bottom lip as I made my fuck faces while he filled me up just right. Not missing a beat, as he rocked my body and I gave myself to him, right here in the middle of the prison yard, not giving a damn.

I opened my eyes after he kissed my lips so gently. I wanted to remember this moment exactly how it was. I didn't want to picture him in his orange jumpsuit; I want to see only his handsome face, only wanting to remember the gentle touches that he places upon my body. Before I knew it, I was gripping his hips and he gave me long strokes. A tear started to come down my face, which I didn't realize was there until he said something.

"What's wrong baby? Don't do this to me, girl." He stared into my eyes before kissing the tear away and stroking my face so softly, so gently, as he fucked me beyond belief. I didn't want to answer because I didn't know if I had the answer. I wanted to seize this moment, so I pulled him to me so that I could taste the spearmint that lingered on his tongue.

I moaned as he caressed my breast through the top of my dress. "Ummm…" moaning out as he bit my bottom lip so tenderly and sweet that sent a rush through my body, I felt the heat that perspired off my skin. The tears wouldn't stop as I heard his grunts and moans; they matched the sweat drops that dripped from his skin. He placed my legs tightly around his waist as we laid chest to chest. The heatwave followed by the shakiness of my legs allowed me to feel weak and numb.

"You know I feel that shit, right? You also know that we don't hold back, right Malia baby?" He pulled my chin down to where I was looking at him when I opened my eyes. "Baby?" he called out to me, placing a kiss on my lips.

Nodding my head, I looked him straight in those beautiful brown eyes. I was lost while watching him bite his lip. My eyes began to roll into the back of my head. "I can't hold it baby, I'm cumming. I miss you so muchhhhh!" I began to scream.

"I miss yo' ass too. You just don't know. Fuccckkk!"

The echoes of our screams and moans could be heard as we both exploded right here on this table. We laid there for a minute as we got ourselves together. I didn't know what to do now because I didn't have any napkins or anything. He picked me up and carried me inside a shed, cleaning me up.

"I'm sorry baby for real. Don't think I bought you here just for some pussy but seeing yo' thick ass had me ready," he explained. I don't know why because it took two of us to do this.

"Baby hush, it's all good." I kissed him after he cleaned us up and we went back outside, going back to the bench in time because Lola was coming out as well.

"Lo, make sure that money gets back in her account. What have you been up to? Where's ma and Cole?"

"Momma doesn't want to see you like this. Cole had to work and she couldn't get off so we'll all be here together on the next visit. I've been good, you know I graduate next semester and I'm happy because that means I'm about to be making that skrilla baby," she told him as her face lit up with happiness as she spoke about what was to come for her.

"Okay, I understand, so I won't say much right now."

We enjoyed each other's company until it was time to leave and then I felt a bit of sadness as I had to leave him here. As I walked to the car, I kept looking back at the prison hoping that he was behind me getting ready to get in the car. However, that was wishful thinking because it was still just Lola and me.

I forgot to ask his ass about the letter, I thought as I remembered what I was supposed to do. Just like that, he had my head fucked up.

Right Hand Man – Dee

I sat at momma Cathleen's house with her today just to come by and visit. I knew after the shit that happened with Duke going to prison, that it was taking a toll on her and the girls. They were trying their very best to be strong, but I know them and their family; the bend but don't break, they were my family and I knew that they were in need. Momma is strong and all she's ever wanted was for her babies to be okay in this world. Duke being locked up is playing on her emotions very hard.

"Momma, come on now. It's gone be alright," I told her as I helped her up from off the kitchen floor. She was silently crying and that made my heart weak. Knowing that she's supposed to accept what has happened doesn't make it any easier. Helping her to the table as she tried to catch her breath, I went to the refrigerator to get her something to drink.

"My baby will be gone for five years. I still can't believe it," she choked up.

"Me either, ma. He'll be okay. With our prayer, those five years will go by in no time," I reasoned with her, at least tried to.

"I think that no good ass lawyer could've gotten him off with a lesser sentence; with his no-good ass."

Thinking about his lawyer, that nigga looked familiar, but I couldn't place a finger on where I knew him from. I needed to get my resources together because he and I have come across each other paths before. Something isn't right about dude and I know it. That case should've been handled a lot differently. We sat around and talked so that I could get her to calm down enough to take a nap. It was good timing when Nicole showed up so she could look after her.

"Aye momma, I'll be back in over in a few days. If you all need anything, call me." Kissing her on the head and making sure that she got upstairs before I left, I remembered to grab all the trash bags throughout the house to take it to the garbage can and sit it on the curb for the sanitation people tomorrow. I needed to go and see my baby momma since she had been blowing my phone up the entire time that I was at momma's house. After taking the trash to the curb, I looked around the yard and her lawn needed mowed along with hedges being trimmed. I made the call and made sure that they came by tomorrow.

Baby Momma @ 10:10: I know you see me calling you nigga. Answer the fucking phone.

Baby momma @ 10:12: Keep thinking this is a game Derron and I'm gone show you.

Baby Momma @ 10:15 Keep on playing with me, nigga.

Looking through her text messages, she was calling my again. Not wanting to answer but seeing that she was on one, I needed to answer.

"Yeah, Naija?"

"What you mean, yeah?"

"Man, what the fuck do you want?"

"Kharisma needs some more damn formula with her greedy ass."

"Don't be talking about my daughter. The hell wrong with you?"

"Bring her some damn food and I need some money too."

I knew that she needed more than just food for my daughter. Naija was money hungry as hell. She worked and still wanted to bleed a nigga dry. That's why I had a separate bank account for her and my daughter although she doesn't know. She wasn't taking from my pockets because I set them up nice. My daughter was only nine months old and she doesn't require much. Her momma has transformed her into a personal Barbie doll.

Looking at the time, I had enough time to get to the grocery store, buy her some food and run it to her house. The grocery store was a good fifteen minutes away from their house. I needed to go and do this pick up as well, hoping that when I got to her house, it would be an in and out situation. At least getting to see my baby girl for a few would make going over to her crazy ass momma's house worth it. I didn't have time to process what had just really happened to my nigga, but I would when I got settled. Running into the grocery store after fighting with traffic for a bit, I ran to the aisle for the baby's food and grabbed four cans. I didn't have time to go through a long ass checkout line so I went self-checkout. There was traffic on the main road to her house so I had to speed through the backroads. Pulling up to her house, I can see that the front door was open. Just as I was getting out of my car, she was coming out the house with my daughter. They looked as if they were about to go somewhere.

"Y'all 'bout to leave?" I asked as I took my daughter out of her arms.

"Yeah, I was going to go to the store since you were taking all damn day."

I hated when she wanted to turn up like this in front of my seed. I didn't know what she was going to the store for when I had just spoken to her less than an hour ago and told her that I was going to handle it and be over this way.

"I told you that I was gone get it and come here," I didn't want to argue with her because I knew how she was. She wanted to argue so she could throw some shit up in my face. I don't know what, but it was going to be something. I played with my daughter for a minute and placed a stack in her hands. She looked like she was still ready to go, so I placed Kharisma in her car seat.

"Aiight, I'll see you later, baby." I kissed my daughter and when I turned around Naija was on my damn back, rolling her window down and closing the door because I know she was about to start.

"You gone tell me what took you so long?"

"I ain't got to tell you shit." I turned back around and looked at my daughter; she walked off in the direction of my car. I paid her no mind as I talked to my baby. Naija didn't understand that we weren't together anymore, but for some reason I was getting all the main nigga benefits. No matter how many times that I would tell her to fall back, it seemed as if she was getting closer. As I was talking to my daughter, I heard something scraping against metal. I turned around and Naija's dumb ass was keying my damn car.

"What the fuck is wrong with your dumb ass, girl?" I jacked her up as she dropped the keys on the ground.

"You're what's wrong with me!"

I didn't even have a response; I got in my ride and sped off. I wasn't about to end up in jail because of her dumb ass again. Now, I had to shell out some more money for the shit she just did.

I was passing Gresham Road when I saw somebody that looked familiar. I did a U-turn in the street because I needed to make sure that I wasn't tripping. If I knew them, I wasn't going to let them sit on the side of the road. I slowed down and stopped after I saw their face.

"Malia?" I called out through my cracked window. She reached in her purse for something, while looking over at the car.

"Dee?" she called out to me. I pulled my car over and got out. Looking at her car, she had a flat tire.

"You got a spare?"

"I have a donut; I used my last spare a few months ago." I walked over to her trunk to retrieve the donut for her so that I could put it on.

"You don't have to do that, I have a tow truck coming." She put the phone up to her air; I didn't know one way or another if she was on hold but I had it.

"Look, I got you. Go ahead and tell them you've got someone to fix it."

I went ahead and started to lift the car up so that I could remove and change her tire for her. It only took me a few minutes.

"Thank you, Dee."

"No problem. You're my brother's girl, so we're fam." She gave me a hug. "I need to follow you to the shop so we can get you a tire."

"What shop?"

"Duke and I's tire shop."

She looked amazed; I guess Duke hasn't told her everything about him. That wasn't my place and I wasn't about to answer any questions she needed to ask him. I was going to make sure that she was straight while he was on the inside. That's my nigga so his family is my family.

Confessions Our Love - Duke

I've been on the up and up while I've been in here. They added time served onto my sentencing, so I was grateful for that. A nigga was really on some mental shit, all I had was my thoughts and sometimes I was tired of them talking to me. I missed my family and especially my lady. Every day was getting easier than the last, but then there were days I felt like fucking some shit up. I had been channeling my feeling into this yoga shit, calming myself down. Getting angry wasn't gone do me no good behind these walls, so I had to accept it and move on. As I slipped on my slides, which sat near the top of the bunk, I brushed my teeth and went to stand at the door to wait for the guard to come place the cuffs on me. I thought to myself how I didn't want to have this meeting but shit, I figure what harm could it do, I'm already locked up.

I was ready for this meeting to be over before it had even begun. As soon as the door opened to the room where the meeting was being held, I wanted to walk back out.

"Good afternoon, Duke," Zion greeted me.

I didn't even know why the fuck was he even here. But, I shouldn't be mad because it wasn't this niggas fault that I was in here, he did the best that he could do and the judge saw it another way. I guess as time goes on I'll be more grateful for these five years instead of twelve.

"What's up, man?" I sat down, wanting to make this quick.

He had been trying to talk to me for a minute but I wasn't accepting any visitors at all. I needed to get myself settled in here and think about this time that I was serving. I knew that it was selfish to shut myself off from the world, but it was best because I was a beast when I first got here. I hated everything moving, niggas were getting chin checked on the constant, and my attitude was all fucked up. I knew when I went into that courtroom before my sentencing that I wasn't going to walk out of there a free man. No matter how much I prayed on it, I knew it wasn't gone happen for me. I had gotten too many slaps on the wrists. I'm taking these five like the man that I am.

"I called a meeting because I think I can make something happen that can get you a lesser sentence." I was all ears; it was the music that I needed to hear.

"How? I'm already locked up." It hit me that what he was saying was damned near impossible. I violated probation and I caught a charge. He wasn't about to sit here and sell me a dream.

"I have my ways. It's going to take some time, but I think that I can make it happen in my favor. I'm sorry about you being here, man."

I looked at him as he gave his apologies while I read him; something was off. There was this glimmer in his eye, and I don't think it was because of his apology.

"It's alright man. This was all my fault and I should've handled my business the right way from jump."

"You hired me and I failed you." He was putting it on extra thick right now. I slouched down in my chair, crossed my arms, and just listened to him vent about whatever. This meeting was unnecessary as fuck.

After listening to him talk for almost an hour, the meeting was over and I was able to go to my room. Passing all my niggas, I was ready to get on the phone with my people. I was going to call my mother first. Making it to my bunk, as everyone went to lunch, I didn't feel like being around anyone so I opted out. Picking up the throw away that I had someone get me, I listened to the rings.

"Hello," she groggily answered the phone.

"What's up, beautiful?"

"Duke!"

"What other the nigga you got calling you?"

"You know I have so many of them that I had to make sure that I was calling out the right one." She laughed. I wanted to laugh, but she better had been playing.

"Uh huh. Let you and all those niggas get fucked up."

"You know that I was playing, baby. How are you?"

"I'm blessed considering, but it's a small thing to a giant."

"My mucho man, I like that, but honey, why are you calling me from a new number? There wasn't an operator on the line to connect us."

"I got a cell phone."

"Oh wow! Baby, you have to be careful so that you don't get caught."

I loved how she was being so attentive and caring even when I could be putting myself at risk. I wasn't worried about getting caught. They found out who I was and I've been good ever since.

"Thank you, baby, but I've got it. That's what I love about you."

"You know I have to make sure that you are always good."

"Thank you, baby, I love that you are so caring to a nigga."

"You keep using the word love." I could hear her heart beating faster through the phone. I don't know if she was anticipated what I was about to say but I was going to say it. I think I was just as nervous as she was.

"I do, don't I? I mean what other words are there to use when you love someone?"

"You love me Zayvier Butler?"

This would be the first time in two years that I've said I loved you to anyone besides the ladies in my family. I was feeling nervous as fuck, but I was definite on my decision. I didn't know that love could happen at this rate, but I spent numerous nights thinking about her.

"Yes, I love you, Malia Olivia Simpson."

"I love you too, Zayvier Derion Butler."

"It took a nigga being locked up for you to say you love 'em, huh?"

"I want you to hear me and not just listen, okay? I was with someone for almost ten years; that someone who didn't gave a damn what happened to me because he was so busy doing him and being with these other females. To be honest with you, now that I think about it, I don't even know if he ever really loved me. I never wanted to feel completed by a man; I just wanted to be an equal. I was never his equal and if I was, he sure had another way of showing it. I know that what I feel for you is real so you should never have to ask. What I feel for you is growing by the day. I'm very happy with you and I couldn't see me loving another man. God placed you in my path for a reason, I can't question that."

"Damn, that was so deep shit. I'm glad that you told me and I'm glad that I told you. I'm not perfect as we can see, but I'm perfect for you. Help me to continue to grow as a man; I'll always be here for you. I haven't had any feelings for a woman since Jai, I didn't know if what I was feeling for you was real or not. I've been taking my time with trying to dissect what I feel for you. Some days I just want to express them and other days, I just want to keep them to myself. You are a beautiful and rare woman; the first time I saw you at the bar, all I wanted was your time. I didn't think that we would come this far. I didn't see you as a fuck, I saw you as a difference."

"Well, it's established that we love each other, just know that I'm gone hold you down. You'll never have to worry."

"That's all that matters. You have my front and I have your back, baby."

"I love you," she expressed and I could tell it was with that beautiful smile of hers on her face. This was my shine through my dark times. We stayed on the phone for a little while longer. She always made shit feel alright in this fucked up world if mine. She could stop a moment in time with her conversation because we were on the phone for almost two hours before I knew it.

Return Of My Past, While I Harbor My Present -
Malia

When loving someone feels so right, there isn't anything that can bring you down. Being nervous when Duke first told me that he loved me, I didn't want to say it to him first until I was for sure about what I was going to say. I needed to mean it and I needed to understand where he was coming from; we had a better understanding. We talk damn near every day and it seems like the longer that he's away, the more we find new things to talk about. Him being locked up hasn't stopped anything, but it helped our relationship. I was honestly gaining a new friend within my man. I was taking things slow and enjoying what we had going on.

I was going out to dinner with Lola tonight. Because I was having a long week at work, I needed me a glass of Patron or whatever hits the hardest tonight. Once I got off work, I was going to go ahead and take a nap.

"Malia let me get those files on the Simon's case."

I had been working for Lawrence for about five months or so. I can say that it was better than working for Zion, it's more laid back and everything flows here. Everybody is happy and they get along with watch other. Lawrence treats everyone as equals and I enjoyed working for him. I searched through the filing cabinet for the file that he needed.

"That ass looks so good in that skirt," I heard Zion's voice behind me. I quickly turned around. What the hell was he doing here?

"I'm sorry sir, but you can't speak to me like that. I will have charges of sexual harassment placed on you," I sneered at him as he held the most perverted smirk on his face.

"I don't know what you're talking about. You're my wife and what I just did wasn't harassment but what I'll do to your pussy will be."

I started to say something but I decided against it because it'll be just my luck that I said something and Lawrence or somebody had heard. Then I'm out of a job, I wasn't about to let him win that battle. Thankfully, their meeting was being held toward the end of the workday so that I could leave not too long after. I didn't want to see his face, so I hoped like hell that he didn't stop by my desk on his way out. I would even hope that I had to run an errand or even go to the bathroom. I busied myself with ads and code calls until their meeting was over. As soon as the clock struck four p.m., I was going to be walking to my car.

Walking to my car, my phone began to ring. "Hey booski!" Sasha screamed into the phone.

"Hey boo. What's up?"

"Nothing, I was figuring that we could hang out tonight or something." I hated to have to decline my best friend's offer, but I had plans. Normally, I would drop what I had going on to kick it with her, but I promised Lola since I had been too busy with work lately, that we could meet up.

"Sorry babes, I made plans with Duke's sister, Lola." I felt bad immediately as I heard her sigh.

"You just done got you a whole new family and you done threw poor Sasha to the wolves, huh?" She laughed, but I can tell that she was feeling some type of way. Thinking of an idea, I hope she would go for it.

"Come with us," I said without thinking, knowing that she might have been against it.

"No boo, I'm good, you go and have fun."

"Don't be like that. Come out with us and if you don't vibe you're free to leave. I just want to hang with both of you."

"I don't know about all that, Malia"

"Woman, come on. We can take my car."

"Naw bitch if I do this. I need my car just in case."

I knew she was dead serious because in her opinion, most females were always plotting and Sasha didn't hold back. I understood her when it came to females as well. I knew that she would get along with her so I wasn't worried.

"I've been watching the phat ass sway in that tight ass skirt," I heard from behind me, growing annoyed at his voice. I dropped my phone on the ground, as he came up behind me. I froze up as he touched my skin.

"If you don't get the fuck away from me." I pulled out my mace and he started to laugh like I did the funniest thing.

"Darling, that shit doesn't scare me." He ran his nose against my cheek and placed his hand around my neck before he tried to kiss me.

WHAP!

I threw up my hand and was getting ready to slap him again when he caught me midair. He then slightly twisted my wrist, with a smirk still on his face.

"Malia baby, I would hate to have to hurt you out here." Releasing my wrist and letting me go. He started to laugh, as he looked me up and down, licking his lips.

"Get the hell on."

I watched him walk way and that's when I picked up my phone. My screen was cracked.

"Hello! Hello!" I heard Sasha screaming into the phone.

"Yeah girl," I panted as I hurried and got in the car. I wasted no time and driving off.

"Bitch, was that Zion's voice?"

"Yeah, that was his retarded ass."

"Do I need to come down there? Where the hell are you?" I could hear shuffling in her background so I knew that she was on her way. I don't know why I wasn't scared when I saw him. I was more pissed because that was the second time that he approached me. He was on some real crazy shit and I wasn't about to play with him.

"Girl, I'm fine," I said, reassuring her because I knew that when and if she got her hands on him, he was good as dead. She had a trigger finger something serious and she was to not be fucked with. "Where the hell are you at?"

"I'm hopping on the highway now." I looked in my rear views and everything to make sure that he was following me. I didn't see him, so I relaxed a bit.

"I'm on my way to your house. I have everything I need, I'll meet you there."

"Okay momma," I chastised her. You would swear that she was my momma at times, but I appreciate her. I listened to the music to calm my nerves after finally getting her to hang up the phone; she insisted on staying on the phone with me the whole time that I was in the car. I told her that I was only about ten minutes away from my house and that I would be fine. I couldn't believe Zion had the damn nerve. He's getting too bold and he doesn't have any shame in what he's doing.

I grabbed something for us to eat because I knew that once I got in the house, I was going to be taking a nap until it was time to meet up with Lola. Although I didn't see Zion following me, I couldn't help but look over my shoulders. I placed my mace at wrist length because next time I was going to use it and hit his ass with my car. Running in and out of the grocery store, I hurried to my car because I felt like someone was still watching me. I sped out the parking lot and went the opposite way of my home. I drove for a minute and I didn't see anything. However, as I looked in my rearview, I noticed this same black car. I needed to make sure that I wasn't tripping, so I switched a few lanes and so did they. I turned down a back street and they did too, I was being followed. It didn't look like Zion's car, so I didn't know who it was. I passed my street and went back on the main road and they followed me. Thankfully, every lane was so packed so that if I hurried and made this light in the turning lane that they won't be able to catch it. Hopping in the turning lane, and doing a quick U-turn, I took a few back streets to ensure that I wasn't being followed and I didn't see them.

"Malia, you're tripping," I told myself as I calmed my speeding heart rate down. Zion had me on edge and now I was tripping. I made it home and I saw my light on so I knew Sasha was in there.

"Honey, I'm home!" I called out as we both laughed. Placing my bags down and heading straight for the kitchen. She had two shot glasses filled with Grey Goose and I wasted no time in taking mines to the head.

"I need all the details."

I explained to her the day of events including at the courthouse weeks ago. She started to say that she knew that he was crazy and that I better had watch out. I was taking heed to her warning because he was getting too comfortable and I wasn't going to be liable the next time that he tries something with me. After we ate and had a few more shots, I was ready for my much-needed nap. I texted and told Lola to meet me at my house and she was cool with it. I picked out my outfit and decided to take a shower now, instead of later because I would be rushing.

***

I was dressed in my black knee length dress that had a split in the back, with my nude suede Balmain sandals. Letting Sasha give me big, loose, and wavey curls in my hair, it hung beautifully over my shoulders. I was feeling the look, so I completed it with nude lipstick and gold and black eyeshadow.

"You look so beautiful. Are you sure all we're going to is dinner?"

"I think so." My doorbell rung as I was still getting myself together. I didn't want Sasha to go and answer it because I didn't know how she would react to Lola. She insisted and I finished getting ready. I heard laughing coming from the front of the house, it was a good thing.

"You better work boo," Lola greeted me with a hug.

"I asked her if all that's supposed to be happening is dinner?"

"I mean I was thinking of hitting a bar or something too. Get out and breathe a little bit."

"I'm cool with that," I replied, looking at Sasha to see if she agreed. We got her vote and we finished getting dressed.

We all had a shot or two before we left the house. We pulled up to the Steakhouse and dinner was very enjoyable. We all talked and got to know each other a lot better. Lola and Sasha got along better than I had anticipated and I was appreciative because our circle was so small. Not saying that we were trying to make new friends, but it would be nice to have others besides us two and a few girlfriends that we have now. Everyone is busy being mothers and wives that we barely get to see them anymore. I was feeling myself tonight and I couldn't stop taking selfies or maybe it was the shots that had me feeling this way. I liked the vibe that we all had together, it wasn't forced.

Pulling up at Harlem Nights, it was packed because some celebrities were supposed to be there. I was ready to dance and enjoy the night with the girls. Bypassing the line because of Sasha surprisingly, we headed straight to the bar. We were turning heads as we made our way to the front of the line at the bar. The men were so into who we were, they never really paying attention to the fact that we breaking the line. It was fine with me because these shoes were starting to kill my feet on this hard ass floor. The sooner that we had gotten our drinks, the faster that I would feel it and the pain won't matter.

"Hey gorgeous," some dude grabbed my arm and before I could say something Lola jumped in.

"Gorgeous is taken, so you might want to back the hell up with yo' hot ass funky breath." She pulled out a piece of gum and stuck it in his front pocket. I laughed so hard because his shit was hot as hell and he was too grown not to have known that. I watched him storm off in the opposite direction, Sasha handed us some drinks and led us to VIP with ease. I was feeling real confident tonight because I had never really been to a club, one that wasn't a business trip for Zion. Feeling down and being submissive for what seemed like forever had me boxed off from the world. Enjoying the many stares and whistles, I walked like the lioness that I was. I looked at my girl Sasha as she strutted the imaginary runway. I was sure going to ask her about her pull because from what I understand, she was a homebody but she's walking around as if she owned the place.

We checked out the scene as we enjoyed ourselves and all the drinks that began to pour in throughout our section. I was flattered but I wasn't about to drink anything from these fools in here, and mess around and be date raped. After declining many offers, VIP brought us bottles from Ace of Spades, Patron, and Grey Goose. I knew tonight was going to be a good night. They played Migo's "Bad and Boujee" and the club went up off the intro alone. This was my song so I was in full flesh rapping the lyrics with my girls.

Being five shots in, I was feeling myself. I kept feeling my phone go off in my purse trying to ignore it, but I decided to finally answer it.

My Duke: What's up beautiful?

Me: Nothing out with Sasha and Lola. How are you, baby?

My Duke: I'm good baby. Just missing you, you gotta make time to get back out here.

Me: I know baby. I will soon, work has been overwhelming for the last few weeks. I miss you too.

My Duke: Oh yeah?

Me: You know I do.

The next message fucked me up and added fire to my flame because it was a picture of his dick. It was hard and was so beautiful as it oozed with precum, and looking delicious. I needed that in my life now, not now but right now.

"Let me find out," Lola teased me as she watched me look at my phone and bite my bottom lip. I knew she could see how hard that I was squeezing my legs together. Paying her no mind, I responded to his text.

Me: GOT DAMN BABY!! (wet emoji)

My Duke: I'm gone let you enjoy your time. Hit me when y'all leave so I know that you had gotten home safe.

Me: Okay baby will do.

My Duke: Bet. Love you

Me: I love you too.

We ended up staying in the club for another few hours. I was way past my limit and so was everybody else, but I had the time of my life. Since we had driven Lola's car here and we were too fucked up, we decided on an Uber.

"Miss Sasha, I know you're going to give me the tea on how you knew that place so well."

"I did the blueprint for the reservations here and besides that I had a little fling with the co-owner. It was nothing serious, only a few dates and a piece of ass once."

"Yes boo, yes!" I chanted her on as Lola did the same.

We decided to go back to my house since I was the closest. As soon as we got in the Uber, I took off my shoes, my feet had to be swollen or felt like it. As everyone filed inside the house, we were running to the bathrooms. Sasha and Lola were throwing up, but I on the other hand had to use the restroom. The liquor was running through me. After helping them get settled, I took a shower and went to my bedroom. Going through my messages and looking at the picture that Duke sent, I called him.

When he answered, he sounded so sexy in his groggily voice.

"Did I wake you?"

"You know I always have time for you, baby."

I decided to go into my closet and grab my rabbit. I was nervous, but I needed him to help me out and I could do the same. Laying back in bed and turning it on.

"What's that?"

I grew shy just that fast. I wanted to lie, but I was too horny to even think of a lie. He put two and two together and for the next thirty minutes we had phone sex and I went to sleep feeling satisfied.

If More Than One Person Is Saying It Then Must Be True -
Duke

"I'm saying though my nigga, some shit just don't sit right
with me. I mean how the fuck did they even know about all that shit
because you only told one person your moves and then that
prosecutor bitch had all the links. Something ain't right, you know
and I know it. You tryna do ya time like a real nigga, but at the same
time it don't make sense. I mean yeah, I would've served the two for
the violation but even that shit ain't right. I mean, you told ya lawyer
so that part should've been covered. All I'm saying is, the nigga you
had was just on as much bullshit as ya last."

Dee had come down to visit me, giving me a few updates.
We've been chopping it up for a minute now. Sitting back in my
chair as I listened to him and what he was saying was making perfect
sense to me. You can't put too much past anyone lately and
especially not a nigga whose ex-wife is now your woman. I just
hoped that what he was saying was just some shit that was on his
mind and not actual facts.

"I hear what you saying for real. I understand that shit
because I've had my suspicions. I just need to figure out how and
why. I mean yeah, I've got his woman, but this shit has got to be
deeper than that. Wouldn't no nigga go to these bitch ass extremes
over no pussy. I see a few niggas that would but that nigga Zion, he
ain't one of them. He has some bitch in his blood, but he can be the
most valuable player to a team. He knows how to work and
maneuver some shit into his power."

"That's what the fuck I'm saying."

The guard called out and told us that our visits were ending. I was glad for this visit because we were still making money and both my family and woman was okay. Nevertheless, I became overwhelmed with what the shit that we were talking about with Zion. It was in my head a few times that he didn't do his job properly because he had some bitch nigga tendencies. I just didn't want to think too far into it. Could I really do anything about it being in here now? Going to my bunk, I was starting to get a headache and I needed to release this pressure. My phone started to ring.

"Hello!" I answered with my eyes still closed.

"Who pissed in your Cheerios this afternoon?" Tika asked. I didn't have time for her smart-ass mouth right now because the way that I was feeling I was liable to hurt her brutal ass feelings.

"Nobody, what's up? It's too early for you to be calling me."

"I was just calling because I wanted to let you know that you have a potential buyer. Dee isn't fucking with me like that so I had to hit you up."

"You'll have to make him fuck wit' you because he's in charge and he handles everything. I'll tell him to see what you're talking 'bout."

I hung up without letting her finish her sentence. I gave her this number because I needed to know what was happening with my business, not for no personal shit. Knowing a lot of shit was going to pop off when I got in here and not being able to do much about it was one of the things I knew would happen when I got in here. Getting together a system so I could still be on the outside was in motion.

I was learning the system and how a few niggas operated. I'm in here with a few people that I did business with and for some I couldn't say that I was surprised to see a few of them here. A lot of them were being reckless with their money, not really knowing exactly who they had on their teams and was just being dumbasses pretty much. I could use a few of them to get me the information that I needed. I needed a few pieces of equipment or at least access to a few because the more time that I had to think the more time that I would get angry. I needed to make sure that if Zion did this on purpose was he was alone or had an accomplice. It was time to go to the yard and I was cool with that. I needed some air to get my mind right.

"Aye, young blood?"

"What's up?"

"Nothing young blood, I saw you had a meeting with that nigga Zion. Just watch your back and be careful." He walked off and I was left there trying piece what the hell he was talking about together. This was the second person to come at me on some Zion's a snake.

Over the last few days, I was wrecking my brain trying to understand who this nigga Zion really was. What type of title does he really hold? The ole head, whose I found out name is Crush, could get me access to a computer ever now and then. I was researching a few cases that Zion had under his belt and his win lose ratio. He seemed legit; maybe it was me who was having a hard time dealing.

Confessions Of The Past – Zion

I was ready to put some fire under Malia's ass now. She was playing and she was acting like she wasn't trying to fuck with me, she was my property and the sooner that she realized that then the better off she'd be. I was going to popping up on her ass every chance that I got. I loved to see her squirm under pressure. I was wearing her ass down more and more. With that nigga Duke being away, I can get her where I needed her and have her right where I wanted her.

As I fed Mariah, my mother came into the house. She looked as if she had been crying or something. It seemed as if she was always having some type of drama lately. I promise ever since her confession, she's been on the go. I didn't even bother looking up at her as I continued feeding my daughter.

"Hey baby," she greeted me while placing a kiss on my cheek.

"Sup ma."

She moved me out the way and took over my feeding session. I was grateful because my stomach was growling like hell. Mariah kept me on the go constantly, but I was handling my father duties the best way that I knew how.

"I need to talk to you."

I rolled my eyes because I wasn't up for this drama right now. I had the day off, but I had a meeting that I needed to get to in the next few hours. I didn't want to regret what she was about to say, so I fixed my oatmeal and sat at the table.

"Go ahead."

"You know I love you."

"Yeah ma, I do."

"Well, your father and I are getting a divorce."

I damned near choked on my oatmeal, knowing that she had to be out of her mind for trying to leave a man who she's been with for over thirty years. I wasn't the nosy type, but I needed to know why.

"What you mean divorce?"

"Honey, you're smart. Don't ask dumb questions."

"But y'all have been together for over thirty damn years. Why would you want to divorce now?"

"Time doesn't keep anybody together, baby. It can either add or demolish the relationship and to be honest, it demolished ours. I've been with the only man that I've known since I was sixteen years old. Being head over heels for your father and giving that man all of me, I've never questioned if he loved me. I would figure that he did since we were together forever. Now being of age, I can tell that he loved me and wasn't in love with me, as I was with him."

"So why leave, after being together this long?"

She shook her head in disappointment "My son, you have a lot to learn. I'm only forty-six years old and there is still a chance at true happiness for me. Your father and I hid our problems very well. It went from tolerable to terrible after your sister Jai was murdered."

Thinking about my sister didn't put a smile on my face in fact the shit pissed me off. Jai was so in love with that fuck nigga Duke that she didn't want to stick to the plan.

"I need you both to get this done for me. I don't have much time and I want to have all of our family business taken care of," my grandfather told us, looking us dead in the eyes.

"Yes papa," Jai responded.

I sat there with a glass of scotch as I listened to my grandfather spew his demands around. I was even pissed that I had to be here in the first place. This wouldn't have happened if he had appointed me years ago. No, he wanted me to go to college and become a lawyer to help the family business. Now this nigga Duke had all the formulas and all the money.

"Do you hear what I ask of you, Zion?" he spoke to me as if I were a child. I wanted to laugh at his demise that was to await him at the crossroads.

"I hear you papa," I responded as neutral as possible. I had to get ready for a trial or two coming up and this was a waste of my time.

"Jai, you know that you need to hurry on your end?" I looked at my sister who didn't look to enthused about the situation as we had planned over two years ago.

"*Jai, you are still riding for your family, right?*" *I asked because she had barely spoken two words.*

"*Y...y...yeah, why do you ask that, Zi?*"

"*I ask because you aren't saying much and you have the key ingredient to this plan. So are you in or out?*" *I wasn't really giving her an option and she better hope for her sake that she was about to say yes and that we believe her.*

"*Okay good, you have two weeks. It's time and we've executed perfect plans. You are free to go darling.*" *He dismissed her but before leaving out of his bedroom, she placed a kiss on his forehead. Watching her walk out the bedroom, I got up as well so that I could leave too.*

"*Have a seat,*" *he sternly said as he lit his cigar. My grandfather was dying from this very thing, but he didn't care and was still smoking.*

"*What's up, papa?*"

"*If she doesn't come through, kill her.*" *He didn't blink as he told me to kill my own flesh and blood. He couldn't be serious, right.*

"*You want me to kill my sister? No fucking way.*" *I had heard enough.*

"*Either you kill her or I'll kill your father and your mother along with you and your sister. We'll all be in hell together. I will not let her cost me my fucking empire, it may not be serious to you but it is to me.*"

"So... let me get this shit right, you didn't want me to have the empire, you never even gave me a chance at it in the first place. Now, you want me to kill my own damn sister so that you can save your empire from someone that you taught the game. If I don't my family is dead?"

"Correct, you were never ready to run such an empire. You have loose lips, which sinks ships. You're a show off and you are an easy target. I always told about your flamboyant ways but you never would listen. Therefore, I had you study law so that you could save yourself. You're a beautiful liar and everyone knows liars make the perfect lawyers."

"Wow," was the only thing that I could say.

"I've given your sister two years to prepare. I told her don't fall in love and what does her hot pussy, weak hearted ass do? She goes and disobey my every command. I can't trust her and something's telling me that she's thinking of revealing my plan to Duke. She's going to die either way. I suggest you jump on board before I have more family toe tags." I looked at him with much surprise, my grandfather was a heartless beast and I was scared for my family. I didn't think that he thought so lowly of his family, the heirs to his throne. I couldn't believe that he wanted his family dead.

Two weeks had come and gone and I needed to be on my game. Today was do or die day for my family and myself, I had a choice to make. My grandfather, uncle, and a few of his workers were inside of his office.

"Got damn it!" He slammed his phone down.

"What's wrong, papa?" I asked as his skin turned beet red.

"Ohhh, that sister of yours isn't answering the fucking phone. They got back from Jamaica over five hours ago, and we were supposed to have everything set." He got up from his chair, very weakly and lit his cigar as he paced the floor. I looked at him as he concentered on something imaginary, as he got his thoughts together.

"Go to the fucker's house!" he yelled with his phone to his ear again.

Me: Answer your phone! Now! He's on one!

Jai: I can't do it. I'm pregnant and I'm going to tell him. TODAY!

My grandfather snatched my phone from hands.

"I told you that she can't be trusted."

"Grandpa let me handle it, please." I was going to let her go and let her skip town.

"I trust that you will do right by me, but I have to send back up just in case you decide to save her. Both of you will die today"

That was it; I had no choice. I watched his men file out of the office and he didn't move a muscle, or even look as though he was going to tell me that everything is called off or that everything is fine. I can't believe he was okay with his grandson killing his granddaughter in cold blood. The plan was to rob Duke's place and if my sister was there make it look like an innocent bystander. But she was mainly the target, her and that nigga. We suited up and hopped in the truck. The whole ride my heart and soul cried for my sister, I couldn't imagine the fear that she must thinking. If I know my sister, she was unfazed and has already repented to her heavenly father. When we finally pulled up, I began to tremble. My body was hot and I wanted to throw up, everything was in slow motion. I thought of my mother and father and how they'd have to bury my sister sooner than expected.

"Hurry the hell up. We don't have all night," one of my grandpa's workers said as he pushed me in front of the pact.

They surveyed the house, tipping windows and doors to see if we had an easier access. Everything was locked, so we moved to the back and one of them picked the lock. As soon as my feet hit their tiles, I felt even more uneasy. I was scared, pulling the mask over my face just as everyone had, we started moving through their kitchen. The television was on, we didn't see anyone on the lower level. Moving upstairs, I guess I wasn't quick enough.

"Ahhhhhh!" my sister continued to scream out. "Let me go!" She squirmed.

"You wouldn't be in this position if you have done your job," one man said as he sent a severe blow to her face that sent her flying back on the bed.

"Let her go man." I grabbed him and we tussled, he pulled out his gun on me. I was stuck between my good and evil.

"Zi?" She covered her mouth as she heard my revelation.

"You want to join her? You know the old man said to kill you if you can't do it."

One of the other men hopped on the bed with her and parted her legs. Her screams pierced my soul. As he beat on her, he raped her just as equally. Everyone laughed as I cried under my mask. Looking at her, she was still awake. What have I done?

"Zi, how could you? I knew that papa would have me murdered by not at the hands of my own brother and just like the coward you are, you're going to do it! You aren't a man, just like our weak ass grandfather and you wonder why you couldn't get his business" she cried out through a bloodied face as she spat at me.

"Shut the fuck up, Jai! If you had done your fucking part, we wouldn't be here!"

We argued back and forth until she said some unthinkable things and before I knew it.

POW!

I sent a bullet to the center of her forehead watching her fall back on the bed and her take that last quick breath.

"We hit him!" someone called out and we all ran down the stairs and out the backdoor. I was the last to file out so I closed the door.

Going back to my papa place, a few people were shaking their heads at me in disgust. We went through what the things removed from his safe and we didn't come up on the formulas, only money and a few of his bricks. Papa was so disappointed that he killed a few of the men. He was so proud of me for killing my own sister. Not me, I was just as dead as she was. I couldn't live without my sister and the fact that I just took her life made me no better.

"Zion!" my mother shook me. A lone tear casted my cheek as I thought about my beautiful sister, but then my sadness turned cold as I begin to get angry thinking about the nigga behind it, Duke. I looked at her feeling like shit because I was the cause of her heartache and pain since I was the one that killed my sister.

God Saw Fit And He Blessed Me - Malia

Sitting here waiting on this appointment to begin, I was nervous and I wanted it to go smoothly. As I waited on my doctor, my cell rang.

"Hello."

"What's up beautiful? How are you?" Duke spoke into the phone but baritone voice boomed off the walls in the exam room. Hearing his voice made my day go from bad to good.

"Hey baby, I'm good. How are you?"

"I'm good now that I've heard my loves voice. What you doing?"

"I'm at the doctor for my annual," I lied because I didn't tell him about the surgery. I didn't need him stressing about me. There was nothing that he could do anyways from in there.

"Make sure you're good. That's my girl, keep it clean and tight." He coolly laughed. I had to share this laugh with him because I knew that he was so serious.

"You know it, baby."

We talked for a few minutes until the doctor came. "Aye, put the phone on speaker?" he told me.

"For what, baby?" I looked at my doctor, hoping that he wouldn't say nothing crazy and embarrassed me.

"Just do it, gurl." I complied to his command.

"Okay, go ahead"

"Aye doc?"

The doctor looked at me with a smile.

"Yes sir."

"Look, I know you get paid to do this shit, but I don't need you looking up my woman's pussy too long. Take more than a minute and you playing in it. I would hate to have to come find you for making my woman feel some type of way, aiight?"

I took him off speaker, trying my best not to hang up on him. How could he tell them something like that? I wanted to laugh, but I knew that would be inappropriate.

"I can promise you that won't be happening, sir." My doctor laughed and I felt a sense of relief as I laughed too.

"Okay baby, go ahead and handle yo' business. Call me when you're done."

"Okay baby." I tried to hang up.

"Malia?" he yelled in the phone.

"Yes, Duke?"

"Don't play with me. What's up?"

"I love you."

"That's my girl. I love you too."

The conversation that we had took my mind off what was about to happen for a minute, but now that I wasn't on the phone anymore the nervousness came back in no time. I waited on the doctor to finally start talking after he looked over paperwork and spoke with his nurse. I wanted to tell his ass to hurry up, but the longer the better. I wasn't ready to be cut open, yet.

"Well, Miss Simpson, I regret to inform you that we can't do the operation."

My heart sunk in my stomach. What could have happened now that I couldn't even have the operation? My palms started to sweat and I got extremely hot. I'm looking at my doctor and he's looking at me. Time seemed to stand still as I waited to hear why I couldn't have the operation. I wanted to ask, but I was scared. He must've sensed o or maybe it was on my face.

"Are you okay?" he told his nurse to get me a bottle of water. She jetted out the room and my doctor fanned me with the folder until she returns. I wasted no time in killing the water.

"Yes, I'm fine."

With a chuckle he said, "I'm sorry if I startled you but the reason we can't perform the procedure is because you're pregnant."

I heard what he said, world stop... Carry on; I knew this man just didn't really tell me that I was pregnant. He has my results mixed with someone else's, he must, he's got to.

"Look at that again, doc."

He spoke to his nurse and she left out the room again. I sat there in silence as I tried to get my breathing together. This was too much to take in, me being pregnant. After years of unsuccessful attempts, God granted my wish.

"I'm more than certain that your pregnant, Malia." He chuckled again as he rubbed my shoulder. The nurse came back in with a test. "It's plain as day, a positive pregnancy test."

"Oh, my god doc. It happened! It really happened!" I broke down crying because I never thought in my wildest dreams that I could have the opportunity to become a mother again.

"Yes, God must've had a plan for you because it was a tough road but you broke through."

"What happens now?"

"I'm scheduling you for blood work for the next week that way we can get a positive in the blood as well. Then from there depending on far along you are, I will get you in for an ultrasound. Sounds good?"

"Perfect."

"I'll give you a prescription for prenatal vitamins and we're all set."

I was so happy that all I could do was cry this was a long road for me. I didn't know what God had in store for me but there are many surprises. I can't believe that I got pregnant without trying when I was told that my chances were slim to none of ever getting pregnant. The tears that rolled down my cheeks were for the ones that knows my struggle, many nights of crying, giving up hope, faith, and leaving everything were it may. Giving up on your dreams, these tears were also for the child that I sacrificed for maybe the wrong reasons, I cried out my repents right here to my Lord and Savior.

Needing to give my Father his praise, I didn't care who was here now because I had everything to be grateful for. Getting off the examination bed, I dropped to my knees.

"Malia, are you okay?" the doctor asked.

"Heavenly Father; I thank you for this blessing, thanking you for never forsaken me. When I've sinned according to your rules. Bleeding the blood over my body and protecting me. I'm sorry if I felt that my faith was tested, sometimes when your backs against the ropes you have no choice. But my faith in you never died. I ask that you continue to wrap your arms around me and this wonderful child of yours that you've blessed me with. Please father I ask to protect those near and dear to me, my family, friends and my foes. In your name, I thank you... Amen"

When I opened my eyes my doctor and nurse were both bowing their heads, the nurse with tears I her eyes.

"Amen, that was beautiful Malia," my doctor said, helping me from the floor.

Leaving out of the office I had the biggest smile on my face. Nothing could bring me down from this high that I was on. God granted me at a new chance of being a mother. I tried to think of a way not to tell Duke that I was pregnant right now, I wanted it to be a surprise for him when I went and saw him in a few days.

Dee wanted to meet up and have lunch, he's really become a new friend my life. I can see how he and both Duke are best friends. They are as solid as they come. their friendship is genuine and you don't get that with a lot of people nowadays. He was looking out for me. I wanted to tell him about the baby, but I didn't know if he was going to tell Duke.

Finding Out Who's Really On The Team - Dee

I was meeting with a new lawyer for my boy today. His momma and I both were adamant about getting him someone that could help. I was going to go to the ends of the earth to make sure my bro is good. I couldn't see him being in for five years, not when we could do something about it. We've lost too many people to the streets and to the prison system. I wasn't about to have him being a product of that shit.

I ride so hard for my nigga because when I was assed out and didn't have a dime that was my man 100 grand. He never asked questions, he was always there. We became friends in the seventh grade and that's been my nigga since. When my people passed away in a car accident when I was thirteen he and his family took me in.

I pulled up to the lawyer's office in hopes that he could help a nigga out.

"Welcome to Collins," she said.

"Malia."

"Hey Dee. What are you doing here?"

"I'm trying to get a new lawyer for your man."

"I have him covered, but go ahead with the meeting since you're here, just don't make anything concrete, okay?"

"Why not?" She was making me suspicious.

"When you're done with your meeting, I'll walk out with you and we'll talk."

"Aiight."

This Lawrence one sounded legit as fuck and he was at a good price. A few people recommended him. I had to give him a try because I couldn't have my nigga in the chain gang too long. He was talking a good game but what Malia said to me, lingered in my mind and I had to give her a try as well. We had an hour-long meeting and he showed me his portfolio, yeah I needed all of that. I wasn't about to waste all my money on a lawyer and he not come through like the one Duke had. After the meeting, Malia and I left out the office at separate times, but we ended up outside together.

"Meet me at the park down the street." I raised my eyebrow at her because she was on some secretive shit and what not, why couldn't we just sit out here and talk? I went against the grain and followed her to the park not too far from her job.

"What's up, why did we come out here and not just talk by your job?"

"Dee, we can't talk about cases or potential clients it's against work conduct."

Feeling stupid, I just let her have it. I guess because I was such a blunt person that I had no problem saying whatever the hell I felt like.

"What's up?"

"Why are you getting a new lawyer?" she quizzed while opening a muffin.

"That ex nigga of yours didn't do his job and I feel like he's behind having my nigga locked up," I told her honestly. I watched her facial expressions and I thought maybe she would have a sour look on her face and was going to try to defend him, but she didn't.

"I see, I think that he could have handled his case better as well."

"Now, do you see why I had to come see about a new lawyer?"

"I guess."

"My nigga don't deserve to be there. Some shit in the past can't be brought up. I mean I understand the violation on the probation and shit but them drug charges. Naw that was some bullshit and I feel as though he was set up."

"You're saying a lot of something but saying nothing at all. Dee, stop talking in riddles," she said to me. I looked at her because she was being so nosy.

"Why are you asking so many questions?"

"I'm asking because just like you and the rest of the people who feel something isn't right, I have the same feeling."

I needed to make sure that we were on the same page.

"You thank ya boy did him dirty too, huh?"

"At first I paid no mind to it. But then one day after speaking to Cathleen and the girls, I think something is up."

"But why didn't you want me to get a lawyer?"

"This may sound crazy but I'm going to work from the inside to find out what happened."

"You're willing to risk yourself for my boy?"

She surprised the hell out of me with this one. She was willing to put it all on the line so that she can see Duke free again. I don't know too much about her, but she was alright in my book.

"I'm willing to make sure that he's treated equally and fairly. I'm going to do my very best to find out what happened and make some shit move."

"You're solid. If bruh rocks with you then I do too."

"I love that man. He's a very good man and he doesn't deserve the shit that has happened to him."

We sat in silence for a while longer as I tried to get my thoughts together. Mainly I was trying to see how was it that she was going to even get around the system to find out. I have access to a lot of shit and even we hit roadblocks. I was going to work hand and hand with her to figure this shit out.

"I will handle it. But can I ask you something?"

"Yeah, what's up?" I looked at her suspiciously, what else could she want to know.

"How deep are y'all into the drug game?"

She wanted to know too much and I didn't know why. Just help me get my brother out of jail and that's it. She would need to ask Duke that because we're closed mouths about our business.

"You'll have to ask Duke that Malia, for real."

"I need to know what I'm up against. I can try to make all of this go away if I had a few facts."

"You never asked Duke about his business, but you letting him fuck on you?" I laughed, from looking at her you would think that she had already done her investigation on him.

"That's neither here nor there. I need to know because I can work around his charges and hopefully get him an appeal so they can release him sooner."

I saw the sincerity in her eyes and although I didn't know her. She was Duke's girl, I still wasn't about to go against the grain. I'll let her know without saying too much. She is the ex-wife of the nigga who was supposed to help Duke get off these charges.

"We're deep, I won't say how far because you'll need to ask your nigga that."

Only giving her enough, she took the hint and decided to drop it. We talked about potential moves and how to go about them first. We were probably up against a bigger monster, but I was ready for the challenge. I would give her a try to help me, if she couldn't then I would have to do it for myself. We exchanged information and we went on about our business.

Pulling up to our traps, I had to make a delivery today. It seemed like the moment that Duke's stepped foot into that damn prison, we've been getting potential clients and I was adding a few more to the list. I had to play it smart because it was only me making the shit now, I didn't want to burn myself out. However, the money was the motive and I had to stack for my homie, so that when he's released we could make some shit happen. I was giving some thought to the whole conversation that Duke asked me before him getting locked up. We've been doing this shit for over ten years, but didn't get heavy until about six or seven years. I'm thinking of stepping down, I just can't right now. I was ready to get married and be a real family, whenever that one was placed in front of me.

Grabbing product and placing them in the bags to load the truck up, I hoped that this nigga would be on time. I sent out a text on my throw away to let them know to be to the spot in fifteen minutes, not wanting to wait. I can count money like the back of my hand, so I knew if we were shorted. When I did deliveries, I'm a two-man army and my partner was down so that left me. Duke and I kept our operation tight with no cracks. We had no time to clean up behind others and we know how to work with each other. We tried to have a few things that wasn't traced for legal reasoning's.

My Past Is Coming To Haunt Me - Duke

"This pussy tight as fuck around my dick. Umm… got damn, girl," I whispered in her ear as she vice gripped me. Her pussy was so wet that it sounded off in this room, which wasn't a hollow one.

"I don't know baby, but this dick is so good that it hurts." She had the look of pain and pleasure plastered over her face. I enjoyed every minute of it. Her skin smelled sweeter than usual; she was so fucking beautiful.

"Do you miss ya man?" I knew the answer, but I wanted to hear her cry the shit out in my ear. It was the way that she moaned, that made me want to deeper than her walls.

"Yes baby, yes!" Malia moaned as she wrapped her legs around me as I gave her these long daddy as strokes. Looking into her eyes as they rolled into the back of her head, I always found that shit sexy.

"You love me?" I asked, tracing her lips with my tongue as her mouth hung open. Her sweet smelling warm breath coated my nose as she panted her deep breaths.

"I love you baby, I do." She tightened her hold around my neck as I stiffened my arms on each side of her body to hold steady. Her pussy was so warm and tight and I knew that I was going to look like a real lame ass nigga if I came too early.

"I'm cumming, Zaddy!" she screamed out as I slammed my lips against hers because she was too loud.

"Shhhh!" I silenced her.

"I'm 'bout to cum witcha, baby."

"Ooouu, cum baby." Kissing me deeply as I exploded within her walls, our grunts and moans made a beautiful symphony. I missed her in my ear, presence, and my space. Wanting this moment to last, I stayed inside of her a little while longer as we shared passionate kisses that made my knees weak. I let her feet hit the ground, as I helped her down.

"Boy, you're so nasty."

"Don't act like you ain't want this shit." I smirked as she did a little twerk and I smacked her on that thick ass of her as I watched it bounce. We had been fucking for the last hour or so in the warden's office. I needed that one on one with her, this intimate like setting. Being able to bend that ass over just the way that I needed to.

If we weren't on borrowed time, I would be fucking those brains out into the wee hours of the morning. She gave me a sense of empowerment, making the impossible seem possible. Her pussy was my kryptonite and once I found out the powers and it gives me, it's like I'm feigning for it.

"I've been wanting it since the first time I saw you," she moaned into my ear as she scratched at my back. She placed a kiss upon my lips as she wiped us both up.

"Butler, in four minutes they're coming!" the guard that I had paid to let me use the warden's room called out. We both quickly got dressed and wiped down what we used, which was damned near everything. Walking out the room just as they were about to come around the corner.

"You two follow me," the guard said as if he were doing a job. I had paid him to do his job and both Malia and I needed to play our parts.

I gave a head nod to the warden while Malia had her head down in shame. I wanted to die in laughter because she was dead ass nervous. "Baby, chill out."

"I am, but I can't believe that we just did that" she covered her face.

"I can and if that pussy comes on a platter like that every time. I want it all the time," I whispered in her ear. Making it to the visitation room with her, we sat on each side of the table. I stared at my beautiful woman, who had this beautiful glow and not because she had just gotten dicked down but another glow; I just can't put my finger on it.

"I miss you and I can't wait until you get out of this hellhole."

"You and me both. So are you gone tell me why the pussy is so much tighter now?"

"What you mean, baby?" She shrugged her shoulders.

"I have no idea. I've been doing my Kegels." She smirked and I smiled at her. I don't know what the hell she was doing to that goldmine down there but she could keep on. I was loving that and I was falling off in it every time I got an opportunity.

We talked for a while and I was taking all of her in. It wasn't often that I got to physically see her although we would FaceTime, it wasn't the same. I needed her presence in plain sight. We laughed, had a few sighs and even avoided certain topics. I didn't want to ruin our time with talking about me and my being in here because what's done is done.

Our visit was over and I was missing her already. Being in this hellhole had a nigga head all the way gone over her. She was my peace through this hellish storm and every day I was grateful for her being on my mental. I stayed in my bunk until dinnertime. Having a lot on my mind didn't sit too well with me. I got down on the floor to do me a few pushups, to clear my mind. I listened to my own music in my head as I concentrated on a blotch on the wall to keep my focus. Feeling the burn rip through my biceps, I grunted through the pain. The last rep was harder than the last and my boys were on fire, but I wasn't letting up.

"Aye, young blood!" someone called out. I didn't look back as I continued my reps. They would have to wait until I was done. "Youngblood?"

"I'm on fifty, count while we talk." I remember the old heads voice.

"Fifty-one, I think we need to talk now."

"Fifty-two, about?"

"Fifty-three, what I told you a few weeks ago."

"Help me out with this rep and then we can talk."

Thinking about what it was that he wanted to say to me took me past my goal of sixty and I ended up doing eighty. I knew that I was going to be sore as fuck in the morning, but I was cool with it. I got up from the floor and grabbed a table to get the wipe the sweat that dripped from my face then I threw the towel on the floor to get up the sweat.

"What's up?"

"I need to talk to you about that fool Zion."

"Okay, I'm listening."

"I've been seeing him here a lot, more than usual and it made me suspicious."

"How come?" I lit me a cigarette to calm my nerves as he spoke.

"That nigga ain't who he says he is."

I didn't want to speak, I needed to hear everything that he was about to say. How did he know that nigga Zion and why was he so eager to get this information to me? Passing him a cigarette and watching his movements. I had to see if he could even get the hence of my trust.

"He is a real dirty nigga. I used to work for his gramps back in the day and got knocked on some trumped up ass charges. When I was first incarcerated, they sent a few niggas in here to try to put me in the dirt, but I knew better than that. Zion was my lawyer at the time and I didn't know that he was working for his family's business. He got me sentenced for a crime that I didn't commit but because I ran with the crew; I was a target for other crimes as well."

"What does that have to do with me?"

"You're Duke, right? Well it has everything to do with you because you have something that Zion wants."

"What the hell are you talking about?"

"I'm not talking about that pretty wife of his. I'm talking about those formulas and the empire that they think you have."

"You're saying a lot without saying nothing."

"Zion is Stephon's grandson and you have what he wants."

I dropped the cigarette out of my mouth onto on the floor. I know damn well that I wasn't set up, how could I not see that shit? Why haven't I met Zion before now?

"I was set up." I reached under my mattress and pulled my shank out placing it under his throat before he could realize what had happened. It was too my surprise because he had one under my chin as well.

"What you gone do young blood?" He smirked at me.

"What the fuck is supposed to be happening next? Tell me everything you know."

I looked at him because this nigga just gave me an ear full of shit that completely came from left field. Here I was thinking that the nigga was just a shady ass lawyer, just to be a shady ass lawyer. I wasn't expecting this shit.

I'm Watching You -Zion

I was in court all day and I wanted a chance to catch my breath, but I knew that it wasn't going to happen. We were having recess in between cases and I was going to try and grab me something to eat. I kept getting stopped on my way out the door, if they kept this up then I wouldn't be able to eat. I needed to get something and fast because I had a headache, from being up all day. I answered a few questions and handed out a few business cards. I was becoming irritated because I couldn't even move a few feet without them stopping me. I was finally able to get out of there and I ended up running into Zayvier's people.

"You didn't do your job. My son will now have to serve five years in prison with no thanks to you," his mother yelled at me with tears. What the hell were they doing here?

I looked at her as she cried and it didn't move me. Who the fuck did she think she was talking to? She had better have been grateful that all he got was five years because I was praying and hoping for the whole twelve. As I listened to her obscurities, I thought of a more sympathetic approach. Something that would make her calm down if possible, because she's embarrassing herself and me.

"I can assure you that I did the best job possible. I, too, was thrown by the findings of the prosecution and they were substantial so there was nothing that I could do. Now, if that hadn't happened, Mr. Zayvier would be a free man right now."

"Bullshit! But it's okay because this isn't the last stop." She walked off with her entourage of people behind her. As Malia walked past me, I grabbed her arm.

"Malia, can I talk to you for a minute?" I asked as she looked at me like I was shit under her shoe.

"We have nothing to talk about," she sneered at me as she snatched her arm from me, which further pissed me off.

"Look, drop the fucking attitude! Why the hell are you here with them?"

I wanted her to lie to me because as far as many people's acknowledgement, we were still married. I will rough her ass up in here or snatch her into one of these rooms if she takes me there. Her best bet is to just talk rationally to me right now.

"Why does it matter?" she walked off and I caught up to her. I placed a business card in the folds of her arms and continued to walk but back in the direction of the courtroom. I had wasted enough time.

***

I watched Malia as she entered the mall with her tight ass jeans on, making my dick hard just from looking at her. I had it worse for this woman now that we were apart than when I was with her. I wanted this woman bad, so bad that I could taste it. I wasn't going to stop until I got her. Sitting out in my car, I waited for her to come out so that I could follow her. I passed the time as I sent a few text messages to Tamela and a few other women.

Me: I want some pussy. When are you free?

Tam: I'll be free in the next three hours.

Me: Cool, three hours it is. Don't call or text just show up. Wear that thing that I like.

Tam: Kissy face

I had a long night last night because Mariah cried all damn night long so I had to sit up with her. I decided on a power nap until I figure that she'd be coming out of the mall. Setting an alarm for fifteen minutes, I closed my eyes as I let her penetrate my mind. I entered a deep sleep on contact.

My alarm finally went off and when I woke up, I felt like I was in another dimension. It was on time because she was coming out on cue. I got myself together and prepared to follow her. The traffic at the mall was crazy as many cars came and went. Almost losing sight of her, I spotted her pulling out of the parking lot. I left space in between us for other cars. I didn't need her seeing me.

"I see you beautiful," I said aloud. As I found myself laughing at her, I had to jump a few cars because the traffic became unbearable and I was afraid of losing her. She was weaving in and out of traffic, driving like the bat out of hell that she always does behind the wheel. We went through traffic light after traffic light before hopping on the highway. We went in the opposite direction so I don't know where we were going. We ended up getting off at Thornton Road exit and as soon as we got off the exit, I lost her.

"Fuck!" I banged my hand on the steering wheel. I could only go in one direction so I took that route so that I could get back on the highway. I would have try this again, I was being too careless. I knew that she could've been anywhere, but I still looked through the traffic to see if I could see her. My phone rang bringing me off my thoughts.

"Where are you?" my uncle asked. I blew my breath because I knew that it was time for a meeting. I had been avoiding it for some time now.

"I'm in route somewhere."

"We have this meeting or did you forget?"

He wouldn't tell me what it was about but he's been trying to have it with me for a few months, but my schedule won't allow it. Not having seen him in months, damn near a year, had me wondering what could he want with me. Having too much on my mind, I couldn't let that worry me. I needed to catch a nut because I was irritated as hell. I pushed that thought to the back of mind and thought of a plan on how I could easily find Malia. Running through my many thoughts, something occurred to me. I could get a tracking device.

Making it to my uncle's house, I hoped that this meeting wasn't going to take all day. As soon as I walk into the office, cigar smoke hit me.

"Have a seat Zion," was the way that he greeted me and I took my seat. My uncle Robert was doing business with Duke and his friend Dee. He was trying to buy them out but he was coming up short. I told him that Duke and Dee came as a package and as long as Duke is locked up his business is sealed shut and Dee wouldn't sell without his consent.

"What's up Unc?"

"I need a way into the prison that Duke is in and ASAP."

"How come?" I questioned, shifting in my seat because I was slightly uncomfortable about this.

"I want him dead, he's caused enough problems. We're still trying to get our hands on his shit and are coming up short. You getting him placed in prison isn't doing anything for us. We've hacked and tried to find his residences and nothing is coming up. Pointless bullshit," he threw his phone down in anger.

"I did my part and got him put away not once but twice." That was my final decision on the situation. I was always putting myself out there for this nigga who just seemed to be so untouchable. He was so far under our nose that he was too far out of our reach.

"Your job isn't done until you've served your purpose."

"What you want me to do?"

"I don't know, send someone after him, anything. But he must die and soon."

I gave him a head nod and I was back out the door. I didn't feel like being bothered with this shit. I had enough on my mind with the murder of my sister. I didn't think years later that it was going to go deeper. I wanted to tell him that I wanted out; I was tired of doing this shit. It was sloppy in my opinion because we'd stop the mission for a while and then years later came back to it. They should've finished it all at one time, our stacks are much higher now.

Driving down the highway, this car was following me closely. I pumped my brakes so that my lights could indicate for them to back the hell up, it didn't stop them. Speeding up, thinking maybe that I was going too slow, I looked at the odometer it read 70 and I was in the slow lane before I mashed the gas, taking it to 80. The car fell back and I thought that I was in the clear.

Boom!

"What the hell?" I gripped the steering wheel tightly.

The car tapped the back of my car this time, almost making me hit the guardrail if I hadn't hit the brakes when I did. They didn't stop and they kept going. I tried to get the tag number but it was a new car with a blank dealer's tag on it. I couldn't see at this time of night, so I decided to go home and check the damages there.

Tam: Are you still coming?

Me: Yes, I'm on the way. Get ready for me.

Now I really needed a stress reliever and since Tamela's exit was the next one up, I got back on the highway and headed to her house arriving in twelve minutes. Looking at my car, it was only a small dent. I can knock that out myself and the paint was still good.

"Come in, honey." Tamela came outside in this nightie.

"Get your ass in the house with that little ass shit on." I walked behind her.

"I'm sorry baby, I was just making sure that you were okay."

She began kissing me. I didn't really want the foreplay, but it helped my growing dick. She did something with her tongue inside my mouth that made me change my mind. Lifting her up, I took her to her bedroom as we kissed like school kids. My dick grew harder and knowing that it was bursting through these shorts wasn't any better. I wasted no time in untying her robe, my mouth watered because she was naked and her body was so beautiful.

"I missed you," she purred, rubbing her hands over my abs.

I watched her perfectly manicure fingertips run across my whole torso and it sent a chill or two up my back. I don't know what it was about Tamela but something made me always want to be around her. Our connection was on another level, she stimulates my mind. But, then there's something about her that says warning. Maybe I couldn't shake the feelings for Malia and I wasn't trying to give her a chance.

Ghosts Of The Past - Zion

Things seemed to be happening beyond my control. If it wasn't my uncle putting pressure on me about this nigga Duke, then it was my mind playing tricks on me about everything that's happened. Today I decided to sit at home and spend time with my daughter. My mother had been taking care of her and Mariah was growing into a beautiful baby. Looking just like her mother, who I missed terribly. Thinking back on it, on a day like today Angela, Tasha, or whatever her name is, would be having my dick so far down her throat as I enjoyed the beautiful view. I missed those times and nobody could match her skills and I don't think that they will.

Deciding on a nap for us, we've had a long morning and I was sleepy and she was cranky. I had to rock her for almost an hour, until she cried herself to sleep. Hell, I wanted to cry with her, being so tired myself. Once she was down, I went to clean up the kitchen and get a load or two of clothes washed. I didn't know that I had my house looking as bad as it was until I started in the kitchen and worked my way around the house, picking shit up. My mother hasn't really been here, so I had to do this myself. My nanny was on vacation with her good for nothing ass. I looked up at the time and almost two hours had gone by. Deciding to finish cleaning later, I hopped in the shower. Being tired mind, body, and soul, this shower released some of this tension. I got dressed as Mariah still slept, getting in bed and closing my eyes behind her.

I was having trouble sleeping, so I took a few shots of Hennessy Black and that helped me to relax. My body began to shut down as I scrolled through my phone, returning a few messages until I got bored with it. Finally, the sleepiness took over and I was out for the count. I prayed that Mariah would stay sleep long enough.

"Jai, where are you going?" I called out to my sister who was walking away from me.

"Come on, Zi." She giggled as she continues to walk, but this place that we were at was unfamiliar. She looked back at me and my sister was just as beautiful, she looked happy and her energy was transparent.

"Where are we going?" We came to a big building. We stood on the outside as she looked up at it. I was still trying to figure out where we were.

"Come on." She grabbed my hand as we walked up the steps into the building.

Seeing doctors, nurses, and patients upon entry, everyone was running around in chaos. I thought maybe we were in a hospital, but there was no name of it on the outside. I was confused as I surveyed the place. Where were we?

"Jai!" I called out and she wasn't in front of me anymore. I immediately started to panic, as I tried to look for her. I tried to stop a doctor or nurse, but it was like nobody could hear me.

"Zioooon!" I heard her scream.

Still not seeing her, I followed the echo of her screams, finding her in the room down the hall her positioning was different.

She was now a patient and lying on the bed about to give birth. She had a big belly that she didn't have before.

"Jai, what the hell? You're about to have a baby?" I looked around like it was a joke.

"I need you to help me, while I give birth." She pushed. She was drenched in sweat and she was in pain. The doctor kept giving her instructions on how to push. The nurses also coached and cheered.

"Doc, how is she pregnant?" I asked. He never paid me any attention, like I wasn't there.

"Come on honey. I see the head; give me a good push on the next contraction."

"Uggghhhhh..." Jai screamed as she pushed so hard. Squeezing my hand until it was almost black and blue.

"One more, honey!" the nurse cheered.

"Ughhhhhh..." she screamed, but her screams were overshadowed by cries. I went to see and there was a beautiful baby boy.

"Sis, he's beautiful" I complimented. Her tears were replaced with a smile as the nurse placed the baby in her arms. She stroked his face and placed a kiss on his forehead.

"Hey baby. I've waited a long time to meet you," she began to say. Then she looked at me. "But your uncle took that chance

away from me before we could tell daddy. Now neither of us are here. You killed us, you killed my memory!" she screamed at me.

Before I could say something, there was this force that happened that sent me backpedaling out of the room. The room changed and now my sister was on the morgue's table. My mother and father stood over her crying. I stood on the outside of the room as my mother prayed over my sister's dead body.

I tried to wake up from this nightmare, but I couldn't open my eyes. I felt myself trying to move but I was lying still, calling out with no sounds. Fighting this urge to get up, when I finally could I was in a cold sweat. Lying next to me, Mariah was still knocked out. I went into the bathroom to splash water on my face and compose myself. When I opened my eyes, Jai was in the mirror with her battered face and bullet wound trickling with blood, looking the same way that she was when she died.

"Ahh!" I screamed as I closed my eyes again. "It's just a dream, it's just a dream," I chanted and when I opened my eyes, she wasn't there anymore. "I've got to get some air," I told myself and quickly got Mariah and I both dressed.

I was trembling trying to get everything together. Praying that I didn't drop my daughter, I got myself together and got us in the car before speeding off like a thief in the night. Deciding to go straight to my mother's house, I calmed down enough so that when I go there I wouldn't look suspicious. I listened to music and Mariah light snores as I handled the car, switching lanes.

"Zion, honey," my mother greeted as soon as she opened the door.

"I'll be back," I handed her Mariah and got back into the car.

I needed peace with this situation and the only way that I would find it, is to go to the place that I've been avoiding for years. I needed to let this burden go. Needing a drink or two, I went to the liquor store and grabbed me some Hennessy Black. Opening the bottle as soon as I got in the car, I started taking sip for sip.

Pulling up to the ceremony as I silently prayed before getting out. Looking at a few people visiting grave-sites, I walked to Jai's grave and I took a seat. I started to get cottonmouth, my palms sweaty, and I was starting to sweat a little bit.

I let out a deep breath, while my tears streamed my face. "Hey sis. Sorry I haven't been to see you." I sipped on my bottle again. "I know what I did was fucked up, but what choice did I have? You went against the grain and couldn't come through. Papa said that if you didn't then I had to do it or else it'll be the whole family. How could I even pull myself together to do that to you? I'm sorry, please forgive me." I took the longest chug that I could without it burning and coming from my nose.

I sat at her gravesite for what seemed like forever; the sun was setting. I needed to get it off my mind because it was tearing me down. I still felt no better as I confessed to her. Being so drunk, I got in my car and could barely crank it up. Locking the doors because I couldn't leave; needing to sleep this off. Setting my alarm for twenty minutes and went to sleep.

My alarm went off and I couldn't find my phone being that it was on the other side of the car. I finally reached it and turned it off. Getting ready to crank up my car, I look out my front window and there was a figure standing there.

"Angela!" I shouted at the figure that looked like Angela. I had to wipe my eyes because I knew that I was seeing shit, when I opened them, the figure was gone.

Can I Talk To You? - Dee

Malia and I have been working closely to get my nigga up out of there. We weren't having much luck now. I only had a little information about Zion's ass like who his parents were, where he was born, and his birth date. This nigga looks all preppy, but he has a record just like any other nigga. I was starting to wear thin and I was going to say fuck it and hire that Lawrence dude.

"What's up sis?" I answered Malia's call.

"I think I have something. Can we meet up later?"

"Hell yeah. What time we talking?"

"About eight."

We ended the call and I was anxious as fuck. If this nigga wasn't who he claims that he was, then I was gone lay a few bullets to that dome. Looking at the time, it was three now so I had some time to kill. I needed to go and get my oil changed. Naija was blowing my phone up, but I wasn't fucking with her right now. The shit that she's been pulling is uncalled for and I didn't feel like rocking with her like that right now.

Pulling up to Tires Plus, I prepared myself for a long wait. I was going to be immobile for a few hours and I was cool with that. I need to sit down for a few minutes and I know that I could count on a few hours of quiet time and a nap or two. Just as I suspected I had a three hour wait. I decided to get some new tires as well. I sat there for the first hour, texting my dumb ass baby momma. She needs to get the shit through her head that I wasn't fucking with her like that.

The door chimed indicating that there was somebody coming in. Just my luck it was Malia's fine ass friend, Sasha. She was wearing this leather jacket and these black leather leggings that showed them thick thighs and nice ass. Wearing the hell out of that outfit, she got many stares.

"She's fine as hell," the guy sitting a few chairs down said to me.

I agreed with him because I couldn't deny it. That way she strutted in those thigh high boots got you lost with every step that she took. We exchanged looks and a smirk and I went back to my phone. I pulled my fitted over my eyes and went to sleep. I was awakened by someone bumping me, I opened my eyes quickly and there was Sasha sitting there laughing.

"That's a quick way to get a bullet, pretty lady."

"You think I'm worried." She smirked and I noticed the beautiful heart shaped birthmark on her cheek. I looked at her pretty smile as she played on her phone. I checked mine as well and I had been sleep for at least an hour.

"Was I snoring?" I laughed because I knew that sometimes I could snore like a fucking grizzly.

"Naw, you're actually a little cute when you're sleep. You're quiet and I like that."

"You came to bother a nigga because he was quiet, huh?"

"Don't flatter yourself I was bored over there."

"I hear ya."

We talked the rest of the time. She had a lot of work that needed to be done on her car and you know me being the nigga that I am I had to check to see if a nigga was hitting that pussy right. She told me how she was single and I halfway believed her because her phone didn't stop ringing the whole time. I peep shit, I just be cooling it. We laughed and talked the whole time and before we knew it, my car was finished.

"Aye, what's the ticket for her car?" I asked the rep and he told me that her ticket was almost $2,000. I decided to pay for both of ours and the total was close to $5,000, but it was nothing to me.

"Take my number." I snatched her phone out her hand. A text came into her phone from some nigga who went about shit all wrong.

Him: I want some of that pussy.

I didn't stop what I was doing, I put my number in there and left out. I had a few errands to run until I met up with Malia. Stopping for gas before I made my way on, I came out the gas station and my phone was ringing. I didn't recognize the number and I started not to answer, but it could've been Naija on her bullshit.

"I can pay for my own shit," Sasha spoke into the phone. I started laughing because she's real high bent over someone doing something nice for her. I wanted to fuck with her head.

"Who's this? I think you've got the wrong number." I laughed as she blew out a frustrated breath.

"I don't appreciate you doing that. I can take care of myself."

"I hear what you saying Sasha and I know you can take care of yourself. You're doing a wonderful ass job at it too."

"Whatever Dee, where are you so I can give you your money back? I don't want you to think that I owe you pussy because you did something for me. I don't want you thinking that I owe you a damn thang because you decided that you were going to try to finesse me. Where are you at?" I looked towards the street of passing cars as I pumped my gas and I just so happened to see her passing me by.

"You talk too damn much, Sasha. You're too fucking beautiful to have such a rude ass attitude, but I like that shit. What type of lame ass niggas do you be dealing with? You talking about paying me back, for what? You ain't ask me to do shit. I need you to watch what the hell that comes out of your mouth. If you want to pay me back, meet me at Legal Seafood tonight at eight. See you later." I hung up on her ass. She was used to running shit in her life, but I was the wrong nigga for that.

678-621-2395: I don't appreciate you hanging up on me. I'll think about meeting you there and you will accept this payment from me.

Me: Okay beautiful, see you later.

I didn't give a damn how much that she tried to flex on me. She was going to show up to the restaurant and I can guarantee that she was going to show up before I had even gotten there. She's probably gone try to chew my ass up, but I like shit that. Not from all females on any other day that shit wasn't gone fly, but with Sasha I wanted to find out some things about Ms. attitude.

I got tired of arguing with my baby momma and I wanted to see my daughter. She was talking crazy talking about how I wasn't going to be able to see my daughter, knowing that I don't play those types of games with my seed. It was imperative that I go and see about her. I let myself in the house with my key. She was yelling on the phone to somebody.

"I don't know what the fuck wrong is with him. I don't know why that he can't see that I love him, Tiff. That shit be hurting my feelings." She calmed down, but now I can tell that she was crying. I picked up my daughter and sat on the sofa. Naija didn't even know that I was in here. She talked for a few more minutes before returning to the living room.

"Oh, shit you scared me! Why didn't you tell me that you were coming over or at least come in the kitchen and tell me you were here." She wiped her tears away as she picked up Kharisma's toys. I placed Kharisma back in her playpen.

"Come here, man. Why are you in here crying over me?"

"The shit that you do I don't understand. You know how I feel about you and you just say fuck me."

I didn't want to be harsh, so I needed to think about what I was going to say. She would flip the hell out in here in front of my seed and I'd hate to have to put her on her damn head for acting stupid.

"You know what this is. You know we can't go back there again Naija, why you fucking shit up?"

She looked so sad and I didn't know what to do or say to make her feel better. I had enough of filling her head up with thoughts that we would get together. When we first broke up, we tried the relationship a few times but to be honest, I wasn't in love with her anymore. I should've been broken our relationship off way long before we had broken up. I couldn't find the nerve to do it, we were together for over a year and a half. That was my girl and I couldn't think about her being with another nigga when we first had gotten together.

"So, we're really over? I didn't want to believe it at first, but we really are over. I see it in your eyes," she replied lowly. I knew that the tears would follow.

I took my daughter upstairs to her room because she was now sleeping and if we were going to be arguing I didn't want to wake her up. I turned up the baby monitor and returned downstairs and Naija was now sitting on the sofa.

"I wanted the shit to work but too much time and too much shit has happened. It's been at least eight months since we broke up and it keeps getting worse. I always want us to be friends because we were friends before we were in a relationship. Can we do that?"

"I don't know about that, I'll have to think on it. But in the meantime, I want the dick since we gone be friends. I can't be fucking you and having a new man and shit."

Just like that, her emotions went out the window. I contemplated on if I wanted to fuck her because this would put us back where we started from. I couldn't deny, our sexual energy has always been there. She took off the dress that she had on and she dropped to her knees, right where I stood and pulled my dick out and started sucking it. I knew that when the knee buckled that I fell for the trick.

After my session with my baby momma, I made sure shit was good with her and my daughter before I left. I don't know how I feel right now because I was still holding on to her when we've been apart this whole time. But I was telling her that we were over and now we talked about it. It's officially over and it was going to be weird. I wasn't mentally gone from her, I always thought about Naija although she was on her shit. I guess the history that we had is what made me want to keep her around. We've been friends and ran the same circle since we were about twenty years old so I grew up with her for a little bit. Nothing will change on my end, that's always going to be my girl. We have a beautiful daughter out of everything and we still have a friendship. I know that if I ever got jammed she'll be there for me with no problems. It was time for me to let her go, she was miserable and she wanted to be with me because she thought that she still that hold on me. I was so crazy about that girl that I let her stab me and didn't press charges after she called the police. I fought her father for her, my love used to run deep for her. Our love was a dysfunctional one that nobody understood. We had to let it go; it was for the best.

Malia: Bro, let's schedule for tomorrow. I hear you have a hot date with Sasha. What we have going on can wait until tomorrow.

Damn! I was so quick to be in Sasha's face that I had forgotten all about Malia and me meeting up. Good thing she looked out on that.

Me: 'Preciate that sis. Yeah, she owes me this date. I'll let y'all talk about me after this date. Be careful, talk to you later.

Getting The Answers To My Questions - Malia

The tension between my mother and I was thick. I wanted to curse myself, knowing that I shouldn't have accepted her invitation to come to my house. She called me after us not speaking for a few months. I haven't told her about my pregnancy, my relationship, nor told her about where I was staying. I wasn't ready for her naysaying and working my nerves. I was running around my home, tidying up. I wasn't ready for her to jump down my throat. I wasn't in that space anymore, so I don't know why I felt the need to get myself together to impress.

Running around my apartment, I was cooking and looking for anything out of the ordinary, hoping that maybe this meeting wouldn't last all day. Or better yet me cursing my mother out, I wasn't for that today. As I was cleaning, Sasha called me.

"Yes, Sasha pooh?"

"Hey baby, what are you up to?"

"Cleaning girl, my mother is coming over."

She gasped with her dramatics ass. Nevertheless, she knew how I felt about this situation and honestly, I wished that she were here. I needed someone to save me.

"I can't believe it but what is she going to say, will she see that baby bump?"

"I don't know. I was looking and honestly it isn't as big as I thought. I only notice it because it's my body. Hopefully she doesn't see it." I looked in the mirror over the tee shirt that I had on of Duke's, it wasn't too big but just big enough to cover my stomach.

"I hope she doesn't see it, or maybe if she does that'll make her get off Zion's nuts. Then she could be there for her daughter and grandchild."

"We'll see, but enough of me, you had a date. I have my tea cup, so what's up?"

I was more excited about her date then she was. Sasha was so closed off from the world because she was hurt a few times. Her boyfriend, who she knew that she was going to marry, broke up with her. She was so crushed and it fucked with her so bad that she shut down, but when my girl got back up, she bossed up in the right way.

"I didn't want to tell you the real reason that I was going on this date. The other day when I went to get my car serviced, Dee was there and we talked almost the whole time that we were there. Well, long story short that fool paid my $2,000 tab and I wanted to give him his money back because you know I don't do shit like that."

I haven't known Dee that long but he seemed like a standup guy. He was sweet and he was handsome, he would be a good look for my best friend or at least some great company for her. He had business about himself and she did too. I could tell that he would put her ass in check with that fly ass mouth that she has at times.

"So how did y'all end up on the date, Sasha?"

"Oh, he told me the only way that I could give him his money back was to go out with him. I contemplated all day if I would even show up. But I thought about it, I wanted to give him his funds so I went."

I don't know who she thinks that she was fooling. She was digging on Dee a little, because she went on the date. Sasha wasn't a go on a date type of person, so I knew she had more than a motive to go and it wasn't just the money. I could hear the smile on her face, but I'll act like I don't just to make her feel better. We talked a little bit more about her date until my mother came over. I started to tell Sasha to come over. I felt like a fool for even thinking about that, I would have to face her soon, it may as well be now.

The moment that I opened the door, I regretted this meeting. I stepped to the side and she walked past me without so much as a 'hello'. I watched the way that she over at my place and I could tell that she had her nose turned up.

"Hello momma." I broke the ice as I closed my door. I walked past her as she stood in the living room to go to the kitchen to get us something to drink.

"Hello Malia!" she called out. I returned with tea and lemonade, taking my seat on the sofa across from her, folding my legs under me.

"You really think this is the best move for you?" she cut straight to the chase, looking over my place like it was filled with diseases.

"What do you mean momma?"

"You left your husband, who makes good money and take care of you, so that you could stay in an apartment instead of your mansion."

"I love my place and like I told you before I wasn't about to stay with a man who had a baby on the outside of my marriage." I picked up my phone and looked through my emails. I really wasn't trying to hear her talk down on me.

"Malia, stop this foolishness."

I took a deep breath after I sipped on my tea. I was trying my damnedest to respect my mother but she's basically saying fuck my feelings. I hated feeling disrespected but that's what it's feeling like. I looked at her and she never blinked with her arms folded and legs crossed.

"Mom, I'm going to say this one more time. I will not be going back to that cheating and lying ex-husband of mines. I don't know what about that don't you understand. If you want him to be a part of the family, make one of my sisters marry his no-good ass. I'm done with that chapter in my life. I'm doing and feeling great. I'm happy ma, why can't you let me be?" I started to cry, these damn hormones.

"Who's the new man?" she taunted me not even looking at me with no remorse like I wasn't sitting here crying.

"You're worried about the wrong thing." I started to wipe my eyes.

"It is my problem when he has gotten my daughter pregnant."

I didn't even say anything to her, how did she know that I was pregnant? I sat there looking at her, not knowing if I should answer the question.

"It's that thug that Zion told me about. You rather have some hoodlum than a real man like the one you had. Despite his mistakes, he did for you and made sure home was kept up. Now you're pregnant by some thug, he won't even be home to help you take care of you or your baby because he's in prison. What happened to you girl?"

I looked at her in shocked. How dare this woman that gave birth to me speak to me in such a manner. She would really want me to be with a man who has cheated on me. I don't even know why the hell I'm surprised. She has become such a weak woman. She knows nothing about Duke, only the things that Zion have told her. My mother couldn't even be happy for me.

"I'm happy ma. I don't know why is that so hard for you to comprehend. Why would you want your daughter to go through that with a man that obviously don't love her! You have become so weak, that I don't even know who you are anymore. I'm with someone who can help me grow, regardless of what the hell you think. Duke cares about me and yes, I'm having his child. I don't want to upset my child, so I suggest you get the hell outta my house. You have disrespected me for the last time," I told her, walking to the door and opening it as I watched her gather her shit. She wasn't moving fast enough in my opinion.

"I don't know what happened to you Malia. You're wasting your—" she started to say, but I slammed the door in her face. I cried so many tears until the point that I ended up falling asleep until the next day.

When I woke up, I decide to take the clothes over to Duke's house. As I grabbed my car keys off the dresser, I noticed the key that I had dropped from the picture and took it with me. It would take me a good ten minutes, maybe more to move around. This pregnancy had me winded most days, but I had things that I needed to get done. I loaded up the car and went to his house.

The mailman was pulling up, I placed his clothes inside the house so that I could go and check his mail. I wanted something to eat, so I decided that after I was done putting the clothes away, I was going to fix me something to eat. Being his closet knowing that the letter was in here with me also had me on edge. I still haven't it brought it up to him, just yet.

As I was cooking me something to eat, I sorted out his mail because I had mail coming here when I didn't really have a home. I kept seeing junk mail with a different address but it was addressed to Duke. I put the mail in the mail pile, and I noticed that there was more mail with the same address on it.

4545 Beecher Place

I recited the address aloud to see if it jogged my memory or to see if I knew how to get there. Once I was done eating, I was going to go there. The wheels were turning in my head from the letter and now the address. I wondered if his baby momma was at that address. I don't think he would be that careless, but I needed to find out. I scoffed my food down in no time and I was out the door so fast that you would forget that I was pregnant.

"This nigga better not be playing me," I kept chanting and wishing. I felt like a real maniac doing this, but I must know. I didn't take these measures with Zion and look what that cost me? Hell no, I refuse to let it happen to me again. My palms were sweaty and I couldn't be driving any slower in my opinion, I was doing 65 mph in residential neighborhoods. The navigation indicated that I was thirty damn minutes away from the place. There was no Google maps picture of the house or place, so that wasn't any help. I didn't care because I was going to get some answers today. Traffic couldn't have come at a worse time, I had only fifteen minutes left and I'll be damn if everybody wasn't taking the street way because there was an accident on the highway.

"Come on people, damn!" I grew irritated, wishing that my Siri had given me an alternate route, but this was the fastest. I had to calm myself do or at least try because I didn't want to have a panic attack, not right now. With traffic moving slowly but steadily, I concentrated on other things like how in the hell was I going to get access to Zion's file?

Lawrence: I know this may be too much to ask but I need you to temp for a few weeks at Zion's firm for me. We're in a tight crutch and we'll pay you double.

God must have heard my cries or wanted me to find something out because he knows what I was about to do. I just hope that he covers me in his blood when I do it. Making it to the neighborhood associated with the address, it looked abandoned here and there with some nice houses around the way. It took me about ten minutes to find the house. There was a car in the driveway and when I saw it panic set in with me. I couldn't turn back because I needed and wanted answers. I don't know what I would say if I a woman were to answer the door, I just know that I find out. Walking slowly to the porch, I started to knock. No answer the first time, but when I was getting ready to knock the second time, the door opened and there was gun being pointed in the middle of my head.

"Who the fuck?"

I prayed that they wouldn't pulled the trigger, I didn't want to die because I couldn't keep my nose out of people's business.

Valuable Player - Dee

"What the hell are you doing here, Malia?" I looked outside to make sure nobody saw her. She had a Glock .22 pointed at her forehead, so the look on her face was shock. I put my gun behind my back.

"Who's in here Dee and don't lie to me?" She started to cry. Now I was feeling bad but she shouldn't have been here anyway. How the fuck did she know about this place? I started to walk out the door and she quickly pushed me out the way, entering the house.

"What the hell are you doing?" I tried stopping her but I almost lost my balance. I closed the door and she was looking around. I had baking soda, scales, money, crack, pills, anything you could name, laying out. I wasn't about to try to clean it up, she shouldn't have been here in the first place. She didn't look fazed by any of it as she took a seat on the sofa.

"I thought that this house belongs to someone else. So this is where y'all handle y'all business?" she got up and looked around, picking it up packages and shit, just being nosy.

"Yeah, now what the hell are you doing here?"

"I'm not cop or anything like that. I was at Duke's house cleaning and such when I checked the mail and it had this address on it. I thought nothing of it until there were multiple pieces of mail with the same address. I didn't think nothing of it, I was just thinking that maybe it was another house of his and I needed to come by and clean it because he's away," she responded. I tried to look in her eyes to see if she was telling the truth but I couldn't read her. I didn't know what to say at that point. I mean she's family and I have a feeling that she's going to be around.

"Oh yeah, this is a house that we got together. Enough about that, so tell me what do we got on Zion?"

"I found out that his family was into drugs. They were into some shit and I don't know how deep, but I hired someone to find out. How they hell did I not know that?"

"You were married to a nigga, who lived another life. Or at least have some family skeletons but what family doesn't."

"I know that but I have a feeling that it's deeper than that because back when we were in college, Zion used to sell drugs."

"How sure are you about him selling drugs?"

"I'm very sure because I used to help him."

You find out new shit every day. I shouldn't have been shocked, but I was because she looks like a good girl. This is the same woman that stayed with a nigga for half of her whole life.

"Y'all wasn't pushing or selling no real shit. Y'all were just fucking around," I teased her as I watched her walk over to the table where I had product and other things.

She went to the kitchen and grabbed a pot filling it with water. I didn't know what she was about to do, so I went back to doing what it was that I was doing. I couldn't sit there with her moving behind me, so I figured I would watch her. She picked up the scale, baking soda, Pyrex glass, gloves, and placed the mask on her face. She handed me as well, I placed it on my face.

"I'm getting ready to give you the perfect recipe for crack"

She coached me through her process of cooking up work. It seemed like she was repeating things that we were normally do. But, she was able to add a few ingredients that made the reaction much stronger. I prayed this reaction between the drugs wouldn't blow up in my face or become too strong. When she was done, I watched her cut it. I don't do drugs besides weed or a bean every now and then. It was the perfect rock and I needed to see if she played her hand right. The look was good if it wasn't smoking I couldn't do nothing with it and that would've been a waste of product. I sat aside a rock for one of my tester.

"Sis, you're legit with the shit." I went to sit down as I let this high wear off.

"I'm more than a pretty face, bro."

She went back into the kitchen and went to work. We had made so much of it, so I called a tester over to see what it was hitting for. She didn't lie when she said she knew what she was talking about. I had one of the best junkies about to come through and if he couldn't get high off it, then it was a no go.

"How the fuck do you know how to do this? Your ingredients go together perfectly and you were able to stretch it."

"I was a science major in school and when Zion needed my help, this was what I did. I was thinking that maybe I could help you. I can help your profit with my product."

"Hell no. I didn't want you to do the shit that you just did. Let me find out my nigga got a real one on his hands." Someone was at the door so I pulled out my tool before looking through the peephole. I didn't introduce them so I made her go to the backroom until we were done. I watched the trip that they had in reaction to her drugs and they wanted more. I had given them a little for the road. They were really on a trip, they couldn't see shit and when they did they ended up going to sleep.

"I told you." She smirked coming around the corner.

"I'll think about it. I'll have to see what type of reaction I get from it in the streets. I do know that if he loved the shit then it's solid."

I went into the duffle and gave her a few thousands, I didn't even count it. She was my nigga's girl so I had to make sure that she was straight. She tried to give it back but I sent her out the door with it. I cleaned up and got everything together for this drop-off I had later. I was sleepy as fuck; I didn't want to go home and then have to leave back out so I decided to sleep here. We had this house laid as if it were somebody's legit home, it had clothes, food and everything here. We always made sure that we had our shit straight.

Me: Hey beautiful.

Sasha: Hey handsome. What's up?

Me: Working and you?

Sasha: The same. About to have a meeting with a client in a second.

Me: I enjoyed our date, your debt is paid. Now can we go on a real date?

Sasha: You didn't even accept the money Dee, so how is my debt paid.

Me: Seeing your beautiful face was your debt to me. I wouldn't ever take money from you baby.

Sasha: I guess. I like that way that sounds. When do you want to go on our "date"?

Me: Is tomorrow good?

Sasha: Yes, I have an early day tomorrow so yes that's perfect.

I enjoyed Sasha's company. I thought that she would be cold and stiff but she showed a nigga differently. She was on her shit and she carried herself in a different manner, she wasn't worried about anything but herself— Being funny, intelligent and gorgeous. I almost felt intimidate because her drive was so powerful. Our conversation flowed effortlessly and for once, I didn't think about fucking a female's brains out. She made the night easier with her laughter and jokes. Naija wasn't anything like her, although she had her own business she wasn't stuck up. I texted her until she had her meeting before falling asleep.

It was time for this drop-off so I hurried and got everything together. Normally these people were on time, but I decided to get there early. Pulling up to the location, there were more people than normal. They looked as if they were having a suspicious ass meeting, so I killed the engine and lights. They couldn't see me because I was in the distance. The dude was having an argument with someone. I looked harder and I saw that it was Tika and Zion talking to that nigga Robert, who we did business with. Zion and Tika got into the car and drove off and Robert went back into the building.

"Hell nah, I knew that I knew that nigga from somewhere."

Since I was early, I decided to call Duke and put him up on game.

"My nigga listen up. That nigga Zion has some type of dealings with Robert and check this Tika works with those niggas, bruh. I knew that I remembered him from somewhere. You know the night that Jai was murdered I was out when I saw Zion and Robert at the dumpster by the BP. They were throwing shit inside of it. I knew it was Zion because I remember those crazy looking ass eyes. I couldn't remember where I met him at, but I remember Jai brining him to a kickback one time before"

"What the fuck you mean? Jai knew that nigga!" he yelled.

"Calm down. I'm working on some shit outchea. I'm gone get to the bottom of it. I need to run this play with Robert."

"Don't do that shit. Have that bitch Tika do it, she said that she had been tryna get in contact with you and couldn't."

"That bitch is lying. She hasn't called me since before you got locked up. That bitch is plotting."

"I know but I got a plan on that shit if it is true."

I was pissed and wanted to kill some people. These mothafuckas were setting us up all along, trying to take what we have. I really need to piece this together and I pray for everyone's sake that I'm tripping.

This Picture Doesn't Fit - Duke

I had Crush, the ole head. come to my cell this morning because I had some questions. I couldn't sleep after the call that Dee had with me last night. I was having a visit from Malia and my mother later. I wasn't even in the space to see anybody, I was trying to control my emotions and I needed to kill something or somebody and fast. Dee said that Jai and Zion have been in each other presence. I wonder how that happened, she told me that she was an only fucking child. There had to be a logical explanation to this bullshit. I was using my resources because Jai wasn't here to answer for herself. I just hoped that she wasn't out here on no bullshit.

"Zion was his grandson and they wanted you out of the picture a long time ago," Crush told me as he lit his cigarette.

"How the fuck do you know this?"

"I told you that I used to work for Stephon, the night of the hit I was there working at the house, Stephon's house."

I paced back and forth listening to him tell me that for a long time that these niggas were out to get me. I can't think of why when Stephon taught me everything that I knew when I was at Georgia Southern University. He was my professor and he saw my taking to science and my growth for knowledge. He took me under his wing and before I knew it, he told me about he has an empire into the drug world. Telling me about the money and the potential, I jumped at the chance. My love for money caused me to drop out of college in my second year. I began working for him, not being a corner boy but making the product. I didn't know what the hell I was doing at first or so I thought, but they made so much money off the shit. It was flying out the door just as easy as it came. I brought Dee on board and we made magic, once we made enough money for him, he wanted a step by step on everything. I wasn't stupid so I gave him a potent recipe but it wasn't my best. It made him a lot of money so I don't know why he would even be tripping.

"Yeah, a few hits have been placed on you. That's why that girlfriend of yours died."

"What the fuck you mean? That's why she died!"

"Jai was Step's grandchild as well Zion's sister."

"What do you know about the night of the murder and how I ended up in jail the first time?"

He took a deep breath "You ended up in jail because of the police officers who was called to survey the crime scene that worked for Stephon. They planted the drugs while they were in the room where Jai was. The night of the murder Step told Zion that if he didn't kill her then he would be dead along with his entire family. Stephon was a cold man."

My heart stopped beating, I couldn't take this shit not today. I gave that bitch my heart and she was out to fuck me in the end. Hell naw, I couldn't, she wouldn't. I don't know if I'm trying to find out so I want to stay clear, at least for now. They called out for visitations and I didn't even know if I wanted to go out there. I did anyways because I wanted to see my momma and my woman. Stepping into the visitation room, they both looked so beautiful.

"My gorgeous women," I greeted them with a smile as I tried to push the incident to the back of my mind.

"Hey baby." Malia greeted with a kiss on the lips. She had this glow and her hips were to spread.

"Hey baby, you look good." My mother smiled as she took in my appearance this was my first time seeing her in months. She was slimming down, she looked happier. I just hoped that she was healthier. We sat down in the front of the room; I was on edge so I sat so I could see the door.

"How you been pretty lady, you losing weight on me. Is everything okay?" I asked my mother. She looked at me with the most beautiful smile.

"I'm great baby. My health is doing better, if that's what you're asking. I'm down 40 lbs. and counting because of this beautiful woman of yours who stay with me in the gym and have me eating right. Between her, Lola, Cole, and Dee I can't eat anything other than vegetables and healthy food. At first your momma was against, but I knew it was for greater good. How are you baby?"

"I'm blessed considering ma. It's hard somedays but I'm okay for the most part. I'm getting in touch with my God some more, he makes being in here with a sound mind possible."

"Amen. But I'm going to the bathroom, I'll be back" my mother said and I saw the look that she gave Malia. It was code for something. I didn't know which look to classify it as, but I looked at Malia and it was like she was scared to look at me. I hope she wasn't on her bullshit too.

"Sup queen?" I gripped her chin. She looked so damn different.

"Nothing handsome, I miss you," she purred with a kiss to my cheek.

"What the fuck man?" I said out loud, looking at the door and there was Tika. I was confused on why the fuck she was here. She walked right over to me.

"Hey Duke!" She smacked on her gum. Malia looked at her and she turned her nose up.

"Why the fuck is she here?" Malia got up from her chair so fast.

"No bitch! Why the fuck are you here? I told you that's my nigga!" Tika blurted out. I see she came here on some bullshit already. She could just leave.

"Duke, why is she here?" Malia asked me as she looked at the both of us.

"Man, y'all calm down," I told them trying to grab Malia, but she was quick.

"I told yo' ass don't play with me about that one but you keep on," Malia seethed while she tried to grab my arm.

Tika pushed Malia and Malia slapped her so hard that she fell. The guards came and broke it up. Tika was hype and Malia just kept asking me who was she, and why was she here. My mother walked back in and behind her Zion was coming over to us as well.

"What the fuck?" I yelled as I jumped at him. This nigga must know that today was his last day on earth.

My wheels started turning, Zion and Tika was working together to get me. Zion was married to Malia and now we were together. I tried to get to all of them at one time before I was slammed on the ground. I watched them with a tear in my eyes, two of the women that I gave my heart to set me up. When I touched down all hell was breaking loose and I was making sure that families got that black on black together. Just that fast my heart started to cold. I had no answers but right now, everything is moving too fast for me. My mother was yelling, Malia was yelling. I tuned them out as I was being escorted to my cell. I wanted to turn around and go and beat that nigga Zion's brains out. Walking into the dome, I saw Crush on the ground with blood coming from his neck. It was sliced open.

"Fuck!" I cursed, I knew that my time was limited in here now. These niggas wanted to take me out. I wasn't about to let that shit happen. Give a body to take a body.

***

I've been like a zombie these last few days. I couldn't even think straight, being in my cell I was becoming a chain-smoker. I had to get my thoughts together. Too much is happening to soon, it felt like I couldn't breathe at times. I haven't spoken to anyone because my head wasn't right. I took a deep breath as I placed my pen to this pad to write Malia this letter. Not knowing if she had anything to do with all of this bothers me, something is telling that she has no idea, but another is telling me don't give in to easily especially after finding out about Jai. I had to get me together and being with her right now, in here, wasn't working. I felt like less of a man and I had to take this L right now.

Dear Malia,

There are some things that's happening that I can't explain because I don't have the answers to them. I feel inadequate and sometimes I feel as though I'm losing my mind. I want you to know that I love you. I'm writing this letter because I can't face what I'm about to say. Looking at you, I know that I won't be able to get the words out so I took another route. I must let you go for your sake and mines. It pains me to do this but I can't see you hurt anymore. I've hurt you enough just by asking you to be my woman knowing that I won't see the light of day for another four and a half years. I can't be selfish and ask you to wait on me. I have to let you go because you deserve that much. Maybe one day I'll be able to see or speak to you again but now, today, isn't the time. I need to get myself together. I hope that you can forgive because this is the only way out for me.

Yours truly,

Duke

Will There Be A Me And You? - Malia

I sat at my desk replaying the events of the past few weeks and I wanted to end my relationship with Duke, it was too much too fast. I wrote him a letter the other day because I can't find my words and besides I don't know if he will call me so he'll have to hear my expression through my letter.

I don't know why I'm getting ready to do this. But there was this dream, a vivid dream of me sending you this so... here it goes...

There is so much that I want to say, but the nerves constantly get in my way

What we have is so tender and rare, that sometimes this dream I can't understand

It's something about you the way you move, speak, listen

That makes what I feel for you seem alright

My mind and my heart is at a constant battle because I don't know if one is betraying over the other but this love that I have for you I can't explain

I'm scared because every day this love is more at a pace that I can't catch, knowing in my heart that you are a master.

A master of a game so cold but so true

That any woman that's falls for you

Is in a world of trouble but knowing that no one can save her but you

So, what do I do with the feelings that have betrayed me?

Betraying me constantly as this love evolves for you

While you sit back and enjoy the chaos that you bring

While you sing the previous song of "I love you too"

But is it true?

Is that really how you feel when you know in your heart of hearts that you want elsewhere

But, is it a shame that I want to play this game too

Wanting to feel you to make love to me, caress me and whisper those sweet nothings that I know isn't true in my ear

I want to feel the warmth of being wrapped up in your beautiful big arms as I try all to crack the code to your emotional demon

A demon that won't allow you to fully love because it's telling you that the right one isn't out there for you

What do I when it's all over and I'm stuck out in the rain, having lost this game. Or worse when I've lost you

Do I walk away before I'm in too deep?

I don't know if I can so can you help me?

I keep telling myself that you are like the others that comes and goes and that I shouldn't be fazed by it if you do decide to go

My mind is telling me that I'm ready for the pain that will be placed upon my heart.

So why do I stay?

I have to go before words get in the way

Let's save ourselves of the heartache and pain

I'll always love you but I love myself more

This poem summed up my emotions right now. I think its best that we take our time for this relationship. Maybe this is for the best, we moved to fast and now too many things are happening. I still love you and that won't change but right now, I need my space. Please don't hate me but I haven't spoken to you and this was my way of communication. Peace and blessings, baby.

Sincerely,

Malia

I loved that man so much that right now it's confusing me. I'm pregnant with his baby and dealing with everything from hell. I need time for myself, he needs time, and we need time. I don't want to walk away from something that could be best for me but until we can figure us out and this out, I have to leave. The way that he charged at us all was intentional. I needed to get my mind together because there was something going on. I was still adamant about getting him out of jail, I was going to do my job.

"You look so beautiful, baby," Zion complimented me. The thought of him made my flesh crawl. Every time he's around me, he's always trying to push up on me or is always saying something to me.

It's been days since I've heard anything from Duke and I think that it was best for me because I needed my space. I think it's also best if we take a break. I just couldn't even think straight, why was the chick Tika there to visit him? I don't want to believe her when she claimed him, but the possibilities are in the air. Then with seeing Zion there too, that day was a disaster.

I've been at Zion's firm for almost a month and I was getting closer to getting him out of there. Today Zion had meetings all day so I was going to try to log on to his system. He hasn't had as many cases lately but all the ones that he has had, they were close together. I was so anxious because I wanted to take this bastard down. The moment that he left, I decided to wait a few minutes before going into his office. I needed to make sure that he was gone. I would have to hurry up and get what little information that I could in a little nick of time. Everybody was on lunch break so I needed to use all senses. Logging onto his computer, I used the log in that I remember.

"Damn it!" I cursed because he had changed the log in.

I typed in every possible combination, until it almost locked me out. I thought about a sequence of numbers, 21413 and it opened it. I went through his files and nothing. Going to his email and he left it open, scrolling through there was emails about cases, plenty of emails to women, calendars, and junk mail for the last few months. January was outlined and I looked for emails concerning Duke and it had his case. There was nothing out of the ordinary. I was about to close it until I saw that he set up for an electronic fax number. I went to his sent mail and typed in the company's name and I saw five faxes sent from his email to theirs. I opened it and it contained information about Duke. I started closing out of everything, but I still had those emails up.

"What are you doing?" Zion asked as he walked into the office, scaring the shit out of me. I quickly closed out of everything, closed out the computer all together before he came around the desk. I quickly got up and I had to think quick or I would regret this later.

"Hey baby. I was just putting notes on your desk and I had to sit behind the desk because I remember the times that we would fuck on this very desk. You remember that?"

"Yeah, I remember that. I miss that shit and you too." He placed a kiss on my neck and I think I threw up in my mouth a little.

"Aren't you supposed to be at court?"

"Yeah, I left Clemson's folder"

I looked around quickly and handed it to him. I put my arm in the middle of his so that there could space in between us. That didn't stop him because his hands still made their way around my waist. I wanted to slap his ass or kick him in his dick, whichever came first but I didn't want to alarm him so I played into it.

"I have to get going baby. Make sure you're here when I get back. I want to talk to you about something." He kissed my cheek as he walked me out of his office before locking it.

Damn! Now what was I supposed to do? I saw him getting onto the elevator and I pulled the note that I wrote down from my bra. I had the name of the fax company; I would just have to get it to

Dee or the investigator. I wasn't about to be here when he got back. Thankfully, Lawrence had sent the email that I was free to go back to the other firm. I couldn't stand being around him another minute. I handled whatever it was that I needed to and I was leaving ASAP. I didn't want him coming back and putting his hands on me. I called Dee and sent him over the name of the fax company; he was going to find out what was behind the fax that was sent. I'm more than sure he had Duke locked up, we were now going to find out why.

I was ready to go to sleep and I had a doctor's appointment in the morning. Checking my mailbox, I had a letter from Duke. Not knowing what to expect, I decided to read it after my shower and meal. I had some Chinese food and I didn't want to ruin my appetite. I read Duke's heart breaking letter with tears in my eyes. He broke up with me and he didn't say exactly why he was just saying that he had to let me know and wanted me to be happy. While I read the letter, Duke was calling me. What a fucking coincidence. I didn't know if I should have even answered the phone, but I wanted to hear his voice, despite what was going on with us.

"Hello." I wiped my tears.

"Hey," he spoke almost softly.

"I got your letter and I'm reading it now. It's a good thing because I wrote you one as well and there are no hard feelings and I completely understand." I spoke words that seemed harder to say, but I had to race through them to get it over with.

"Look, I can't explain shit right now, but I have to let you be free at least for now. What was your letter about?"

"I matched what you were saying. I agree with you and it's best that we do part ways."

"So, that's it on us, huh?"

"I guess so."

This conversation was now awkward and I didn't know if I wanted to sit on the phone with him anymore. I let my tears silently fall as we held the phone for what seemed like an eternity. I wanted him to hold me, and I wanted us to be okay. It was too much damage and I don't think we can come from back from it. I don't even know what happened and I hope that he didn't cheat on me. I was now officially single again.

Love All Over Me – Malia

4 months later

We hadn't heard anything yet about the judge's decision on the retrying of Duke's case. We hired Lawrence and we had a fighting chance. He told us that our chances were greater for them to overturn the case. I couldn't wait until he had court again, I was ready for him to come home. I haven't spoken to him since our break up, but I can't help how I feel for him. I was putting myself out there, I helped Dee make more profit for their business and I was fighting for him chance at freedom.

I called Dee and asked him to come to the doctors with me. I wasn't feeling too well this morning. Sasha was busy with work and I didn't have anyone to go with me.

"You look bad as hell, sis."

"I know, I don't feel good at all and I wanted to have the doctor catch whatever this is before the baby catches it."

He looked at me, I guess I hid my bump well.

"You're pregnant? Why the hell didn't you tell me?"

"I didn't know the right words to say, Dee. This pregnancy has been hidden for a while, I wanted to tell Duke but you know our break up didn't make it easier for me. I'm trying to remain stress free. You understand, right?"

"I understand that sis, but we're family and we're here for each other. I'm here for you."

"Thank you, bro."

I was glad that I had finally told him. He deserved to know just as much as Duke did, which was why I was going to see him today. I know that we broke up but I still wanted to include him on the baby. I was being selfish by not telling him in the first place, I thought that I was doing him good by not saying anything. I just didn't want to add any more stress on him; he has enough going on.

The doctor did an ultrasound on me. I was just at the five-month mark with being pregnant and he asked if I wanted to know the sex, in my heart I knew that I was having a boy. It wouldn't necessarily hurt me if I wasn't. I decided to do a surprise gender reveal, baby shower, so I opted out of the sex. As I was leaving from my appointment, Dee went back inside to ask my doctor a question; not saying exactly what it was I dropped the situation. I dropped Dee off at his house and Sasha had gotten off work early so she was going to go with me to see Duke. I was glad that she agreed because I didn't want to drive an hour out by myself, I get tired too easily.

The whole ride Sasha and I reminisced on our college days. We used to be some wild ass females, I was reserved, but I had that ratchet streak that I allowed to overshadow on a few occasions. I'm glad that I allowed myself to open after being with Zion all those years, I f I wasn't then I wouldn't have gotten the opportunity to meet Duke.

"Are you ready to be a mommy?" she excitedly asked me.

"I am, but I will feel better when I tell Duke about the baby."

"You miss him, don't you?"

"You know I do. More than anything, that man has shown me a new meaning of love. He taught me that everything isn't perfect and mistakes are okay."

"Sis, this love has made you grow. Although you aren't together, you still love him. There's a real difference between your love with Zion and your love with Duke."

"This love is exhilarating, I can't explain it, but I've got love all over me baby." I smiled so brightly.

We pulled up to the prison and I was so nervous, like the first time that I went to visit him. That man did something to me that I couldn't put into words. We were broken up and a mutual one at that and I still loved him. In fact, I think I may love him now more than anything. Loving him comes without limits and I was okay with that. I was tired of trying to control everything in my life, but at the same time I couldn't control how he felt. Not having talked to him but maybe a once after our breakup gave me time to think and I may have overreacted to the situation with that Tika bitch. He and I were going to have to talk out or problems and today was the day. We did the original protocol so that we could go to the visitation room. I sat there with butterflies in my stomach.

"Woman, stop shaking like that." Sasha rubbed my back to calm me down.

"I can't, I don't know why but I'm nervous to see him."

"If loves has you like that, I'm good on that shit." She laughed. I gave her the side eye, she knew that she wanted this too.

"We'll talk about that later."

I watched the clock on the wall and twenty minutes had passed by and Duke hadn't come out with everyone else, all the inmates come out together.

"Excuse can you tell me where Zayvier Butler is?"

"Duke?" he asked, I guess they learned who he was.

"Yes, oh he was transferred a few weeks ago"

"Where?" I was now nervous because he couldn't call me to tell me that he was leaving here.

"You'll have to get that information from the front desk."

I walked out of there was fast that I left Sasha. Finding my way to the front, I wasted no time in asking question after question. I was informed that they couldn't give me any information because he was no longer an inmate at their facility.

"It's okay baby. Maybe he needs to get into the system and then he'll call you."

I tried to reason with her logic but I wasn't easy about it. Not knowing where he was I didn't know what to think. I didn't want to call his mother yet because I'm sure nobody knows. I decided to send Lola a text and she told me that she hasn't heard from him weeks.

"Dee and I have been seeing a lot of each other." Sasha tried to change the subject and I knew that she was trying to keep my mind off things. I wasn't going to ruin her moment because she was happy when she spoke of Dee.

"I know y'all have. That smile is so bright boo, let me find out you are serious about him."

"I think we may be. I'm scared and you know how I feel about relationships."

"I know boo but this could be a good thing. Sasha, don't ruin something with potential with your thoughts. You overthink things and I know how you are."

"I can admit that we have a great time together."

The rest of the ride was us talking about relationships. Sasha and Dee was a nice couple for each other. His baby mom took a lot out of him and that's why he was fucking anything moving. Sasha was afraid of commitment because the one that she loved left her without so much as to a why. Nevertheless, I can admit it helped me to not worry about Duke for a while. I knew that he was safe, I just prayed over him.

Grant Me This One Prayer - Duke

1 ½ months later

I had been praying that these people would see me again. After the first denial for an appeal, I didn't think that I would get another chance. I wasn't giving up, I was going to be fighting for my freedom even if it took me the next four and a half years. Waking up with high hopes on things going my way with this hearing, I wanted to at least get a fair chance in the game. I knew that my chances of getting an appeal were slim to none, but slim was better than none. I wanted to tell them about that snake ass lawyer that I had, but I wasn't a snitch and he was going to get his. Sitting on the edge of my bunk just thinking about the shit that I've been through up until this moment, I promise that a nigga was supposed to have been broken by now. I just couldn't though, I had to be strong for the ones on the outside.

"Duke, it's time to go!" the guard called out.

I straightened out the small wrinkles in prison shirt and pants along with brushing off my lent. I needed my appearance to be up to par, because they look at all of that. I needed them on my side today, just for today. I kissed my bible before leaving my cell. As I walked out the cell and through the domes, everyone said their well wishes and all that other shit that you say to someone but don't mean it. I could use it from the genuine ones, but that was the least of my worries. I had to wait until it was time for my hearing and I was more anxious with every minute. When it was my time, I was just as nervous; I needed this to work in my favor. Looking at the counsel as they looked over me and the files that contained a lot of shit about myself, knowing that they were judging me based on the thick ass files.

"We hear by grant your motion for an appeal."

I think my heart stopped when I heard her tell me that. I stand before them in this a prison clothes with tattoos showing and a long beard. They see me nothing more than a thug. Dropping to my knees I had to give the man upstairs of all his praises.

"Heavenly Father,

I knew you would never forsake me. I never doubted you, I bleed your blood and I am your son. I'm a believer and an overcomer and don't know what it is that you're doing in my life. But, I believe that this time here was meant for me for a reason because you're working. I hear you. In your name, thank you… Amen."

I wiped the tears from my eyes, I looked at the board and a few of them were wiping away their tears as well. I didn't care at that moment, I was very grateful that they were even trying to hear a nigga out, after being denied before.

***

The appeal went well and a nigga was going to be free soon. I had a lot on my mind and I had some shit to do. That nigga Zion wouldn't breathe another fucking piece of air when they release me from this cage. I missed my family and Malia, who has been on my mind constantly although we parted ways. This time away had my heart fucked up, but I was in love with her and spending time away from her made me see just that. I wanted to start a family with her, move on, and start over. I wasn't letting anybody know that I was coming home because I wanted it to be a surprise, I let Dee know because I wanted him to pick me up whenever they released me. I was going to go about my regular routine until the day that the opened up this cage and set me free.

"Forty-seven, forty-eight, forty-nine, fifty," I counted as I did my sit-ups. I was releasing this stress and just passing time until it was time for me to get up out of here. I had been doing a lot of reading and I came across this author named A. Ward, his pen game was on point. After I read his book Bad For You: A Gangster's Mantra, I saw some of the shit that Bo went through and I could relate. I started to write a little of my own, since I couldn't really paint how I wanted, I used my pen to create a masterpiece.

"Aye Duke!" Spoony called out. He was in here on two murder charges walked up to my cell.

"What's up?"

"I heard you're getting out soon; hook me up when you get out."

I really hated that niggas knew what I was in here for; they talked worse than bitches from the police station to the jailhouse. When I first got in here, I thought about drugs a lot because I was thinking of all the money that I was going to lose while I was away. I would just have to hit the ground running when the time came. I didn't want to discuss this shit with him. Although he was a cool ole head, I was still reserved.

***

Hearing my cell door opening made a nigga feel alive again. I didn't even mind going through the long ass process of getting out. I was going to wait if it meant that I was free.

"Damn nigga, you got swoll as fuck in there," Dee greeted me as he gave me a brotherly hug.

"You know how it is, all you can do is either starve, eat that nasty ass food, or workout." I flexed my muscle.

"Nigga, you're 'bout to bust clean out of those little ass clothes. Let's get you up out of here."

He hopped in the passenger seat and left me outside. I looked at that nigga like he had lost his mind as I admired the matte black Mercedes G-Wagon that he pulled up in. I think he was on a bean or something because there was no way in hell that I'll be driving away from this prison just to get stopped and booked again.

"Get yo' ass in the driver's seat. I'm tired as fuck." He laughed and let the window back up. Nothing has changed with my boy at all; still rude as hell. I stood there and laughed, I missed my nigga. But, I was going to stand here until his ass got back in the driver's seat.

"Nigga, I'm not about to be driving off these folks' property. You're tryna send a nigga back in, huh?" I stood there trying to argue with his silly ass. He threw something at me and let the window back up. I opened my wallet and it had everything in it that I left in there over a year ago. Not wanting to waste any more time, I just hopped in the car. Hopping behind the wheel and adjusted what I needed, I pulled off. Enjoying the privilege of being able to drive again, we had a while before we had even gotten close to Atlanta, but I was going to enjoy this drive. I had my freedom back and I couldn't hide the happiness that I felt. It seemed like forever since I've seen the city, any city, and multiple people besides hard legs and ugly ass correctional officers. Looking to my right Dee was knocked out, so it was only me asnd the roads. I turned up the radio and just cruised, laughing at my recent events.

"Heavenly father, thank you for this blessing."

I finally hit 75 and Dee had woken up. We still had another thirty minutes or so before we pulled up to his house, I guess if he still stayed there.

"Nigga, we ain't there yet?"

I laughed at him because he was still impatient as ever.

"Naw nigga, where am I going?"

"Take me to my spot."

He lit a blunt and the smell made me stomach smile. I missed this shit, and since I wasn't on papers I was going to take full advantage of it. Placing the blunt up to my lips, I inhaled and savored every taste of it.

"Yeaaaah nigga, that's that new shit," Dee gloated as he monitored my motions as I smoked. I began to cough. "Hell yeah, I know that shit is smokin' if you're choking, but then again you got them baby ass lungs now." He died in a pit of laughter.

"This shit is hittin', nigga" I passed it back while I tried to catch my breath.

"I know. This that Diamond Rust." He inhaled the blunt as he chilled, while examining his work.

"That shit strong is as fuck. I know you're pushing that, right?"

"Naw, I wanted to wait until you got home before I did that. This is something special and I need to make sure I got my boys opinion first. I had to play with it a few times because it wasn't balanced. When I first tried it, I started tripping hard as hell, nigga."

I didn't want to laugh but he way that this nigga was looking at the blunt as he spoke was almost like he was scared to smoke it some more.

"Well, it's gotten my approval. Let's get this shit in the streets."

We finally pulled up to his spot but instead of him living in his original spot, he got the house down the street. It was a nice mansion, I never understood why this nigga had big houses and it was only him that stayed there. He wasn't up for visitors and don't really have family besides mine since his folks died years ago. He started to get out the car and I followed.

"Naw, nigga go home." He laughed, stopping me from getting out the car.

"You gotta take me, dumb ass nigga."

"No I don't. You have yo' car." He laughed.

"Nigga what?" I looked outside the car to see if any of my whips were in his driveway and I saw none, so I was confused.

"This is yo' truck, nigga." He laughed, pulling out all the registration. Looking over the paperwork, this car was registered to me. I wasn't ready to get emotional and shit, so I brushed it off.

"'Preciate this shit, bruh." I dapped him up and he got out the car.

"I'll be by later. I need to get some sleep."

"Bet."

Cruising my city streets, I made my way to my house. My city was looking even more beautiful in this new freedom that I had. A tear or two dropped because I couldn't hold my composure, thinking about how I wasn't supposed to be here until another four years from now. I didn't even mind sitting in traffic, I was grateful and I couldn't express it enough.

Finally pulling up, I smiled because I thought I wouldn't this place again. I sat in the street looking at my house with a smile, this was home and I'm more appreciative of it now more than anything. When I pulled up in the driveway, I just sat in the whip, saying a silent prayer. When I got out of the car, I stood there for a minute to take it all in.

"You're lucky man," I said aloud.

Opening the door to the aroma of vanilla, it made me feel right at home. Heading straight for the kitchen, I went to the refrigerator, which was stocked, nice and neat. I grabbed a PowerAde before heading up to my room. My bedroom suit was changed from the chocolate to now black and gold. It was on some king shit and I was digging it. I looked around a bit before I decided to hop out of these little ass clothes and put some real soap on my balls. Turning on my music and let the sounds of Anita Baker fill the room. I let the triple showerhead run over me as I washed my body and hair, letting the water run until it started to get cold. Deciding to lay in bed just as naked as a nigga was born, I was about to enjoy this sleep until tomorrow. Nobody knew that I was home, so I was going to do my pop ups tomorrow and during the rest of the week.

Making Her My Woman And Starting A New - Dee

I was going to ask Sasha to be mines since we've been dating for over a few months.

"Got damn!" I looked over her body as the outfit she had on looked painted on her thick curves. Her fragrance filled the room and I couldn't stop staring. Her beautiful curly mane was what set it off for me.

"Hey boo." She hugged me and I let the hug linger as I held her soft body in my arms.

"Are you ready to go?"

"I was thinking that maybe we could have dinner here."

"Why you didn't tell me? I could've dressed down." I looked over the suit that I had on.

"I thought of it at the last minute. I would like to spend an evening with you, alone."

"I'm cool with that but a nigga is uncomfortable in this outfit."

"You can change if you want."

I ran outside and got my gym bag out the car. I had some clean ball shorts and a tee shirt with a pair of Jordan's in there as well. When I came back from the bathroom, Sasha was sitting on the couch in some pajamas, her makeup was off and she looked even more beautiful without it.

"I'd rather watch Netflix and eat popcorn. I love the restaurants, but sometimes I could do without that, a nice night at home is always good too. Sometimes being in is better than being out."

"I like that. I'm cool with it as long as you are. I'm moving on your time and if this is what you want then I'm all in."

"I took my time with this process. I had to make sure that I wanted to invite you into that part of my life. We haven't even had sex yet and I feel like I have this mental connection with you."

I was feeling everything that she was saying, I'm glad that we haven't taken it there. Getting to know her on more than the physical. I loved our energy, I liked her presence and her company.

"I do too. I appreciate the woman that you are because you took me to a new level with my thinking of women. Women see me and all they see is money. All I was doing was fucking and leaving them. My baby momma and I had a toxic ass relationship, but we made something so beautiful from our organized chaos. My daughter is the best thing that has happened to me and I'm thankful to her mother for giving her to me. Does me having a child bother you?"

"I haven't said anything before now and I won't say anything because I can't do anything about that. Your daughter is a part of you and if you're going to be in my life then she will too.

"You want a nigga in your life, huh?"

"I do. I'm ready to take a chance on you. I don't know where we're going to go with this, but I'm willing to try. I like who I am when I'm with you, I am myself and you're a man that takes charge."

We talked about the possibilities of our relationship. I looked at this as a learning experience; I felt that I was finally doing something right. Sasha made a nigga feel good about himself. She kept me on my toes and I enjoyed that she was a challenge. We ate popcorn and chilled with Netflix, I was enjoying this moment because it was rare that I had even gotten to this point with a female without fucking her before the credits.

She curled under me and I hugged her tightly. "This is nice," she told me halfway through the movie.

"It is for real, you making a nigga watch Netflix and I'm being able to sit through the movie without other shit happening."

"I didn't say anything wasn't going to happen." I smirked as she kissed me.

She started to straddle my lap as I held her around her thick waist. The smell of her perfume lingered in between the both of us. She let her hands roam over my chest as I let my hands roam over her thick physique. The way that we were kissing you would swear that we were sexually deprived.

"You sure you want this to happen?"

"If I wasn't then you wouldn't be here, we wouldn't be here."

"I hear what you're saying and don't get me wrong. I want this to happen, but I need to talk to you first."

She adjusted herself on my lap and now I had her undivided attention. The way that her face held her blank expression let me know that she thinks that I'm about to come at her on some bullshit, but I was about to come at her on the exact opposite.

"Say what you have to say, Dee"

"Hold on. Don't think I'm on some bullshit, I think that we should take this relationship to another level."

"What do you mean?"

"I was thinking that you and I can finally make this relationship official."

"I was thinking the same thing."

"I'm serious; I'm thinking that we'll be good together."

"Me too."

Instead of us fucking, we stayed up and talked all night. For the first time in a long time, I felt a connection with a female besides sexually. She learned and studied me the way that no female has ever had. We made our relationship official and we were going to take it day by day. We were going to build instead of just jumping right in.

The next morning when we woke up, I caught her coming out of the bathroom as water dripped from her body, and I wanted to slide up through her. I don't know if she was trying to try me with this lame shit, but the smirk on her face told me that she was doing it intentionally.

"You wanna play, huh?"

"What are talking about, babe?"

"So, you just coincidentally just decided to take a shower and bring your ass in here like that?"

"Boy bye, I wasn't thinking about you. I wanted to clean my pussy that's all."

"Yeah, I hear you but where are you your toothbrushes and shit so I can get this dragon out my mouth." I went into the bathroom and decided to handle my hygiene before my shower. I took my time because I knew she tried to play a dirty game when she came out naked and shit. I wrapped my towel around my waist and went into her bedroom.

She choked on her water, when she saw me.

"You alright, baby?" I patted her back as she tried to catch her breath.

"Yes... cough... I... cough... am." She looked at me and stood up from the bed quickly. I smirked because her eyes got bucked when she saw my dick. I wasn't about to play with her, but I could play her games.

"Are you sure?"

She got back on the bed and pulled at my towel. There was so much going on and it was happening at a reasonable speed. We touched and felt on each other, practiced 69, and then it went down. The way that we fucked on each other, we gave each other a run for our money. She made my toes curl the way she did her thing. I was going to enjoy being with someone who enjoy me as a man and not anything other than that.

I Thought The I'd Never See You Again - Duke

I had been low key ever since I had been released, I spent the first few days in the house enjoying the peace and quiet. I never knew how much I missed something until I didn't have it in my possession anymore. I was liking what my mother and sisters had done to the place. I hopped in the shower so that I could get ready to leave out. Somebody was coming in my house, all I had on was my towel and my body was still dripping wet. I grabbed my gun, and went downstairs. I kept quiet because I needed to hear their movements. They were in my kitchen, so I went down. I prayed that I didn't have to catch a body.

"Who the fuck?"

I came around the corner.

"Oh my god!" Malia screamed as she dropped the carton of orange juice on the floor.

"Malia?" I looked at her, but what caught me was her big ass stomach.

"Duke!" she screamed running over to me. "What are you doing home?"

"I was released a few days ago. What are you doing here?"

"I've been coming by and cleaning your home since you've been away."

I smiled at her, but I was nervous because she was obviously carrying a baby. I didn't know if it were mine or not, I prayed that it was. I didn't know how to come at the situation.

"Thank you so much. I knew it had a specific touch, I just couldn't place it."

"Yeah, when I got lonely at my home, I would come here to sleep just so that I could be close to you," she cried and I hated to be the reason for these tears.

"I'm sorry, I had to go away baby, but I'm home now."

I walked us out of the kitchen and into the living room; I went to my laundry room and grabbed a pair of boxers and ball shorts. I looked at this beautiful woman who glowed so radiantly and she was getting ready to be a mother. That was such a beautiful gift.

"I didn't know that I would see you again before four years."

"I know. I don't even know what to say. I didn't expect to see you so soon."

"I know and there's so much that I wanted to say to you, but not knowing how because the last time we spoke was months ago and we had broken up."

"Understandable." I nodded because I didn't know what to say. I wanted to ask the obvious. "So, what's been up?"

"Just carrying a baby and working."

"I see and you look so beautiful."

"Thank you, I can thank you for that."

"Me?" She nodded as she smiled. "That's my baby?" I asked stupidly.

"Yes, I believe that it's a boy. I'm not sure though."

"My son, huh?" My heart fluttered as I repeated those words. The thought of possibility of having a son made me smile. Whether it's a girl or boy, I was going to be a father and that's all that matters.

"I'm sorry; I wanted to tell you about the baby when I saw you last, but so much happened that day."

"I'm sorry about that too. I have some shit to make happen on that end."

"Were you sleeping with her?"

"Who Tika? Fuck outta here, Malia. I told you that I'm a solid nigga. I don't do that fucking around, especially not on the woman that I fucking love."

"I had to ask. I have a question and I want you to be honest with me, Duke."

"Okay Malia, what's up?"

I watched her walk off and walked upstairs. I knew the struggle that she was having going up and down the stairs so I went up behind her. She was in my closet; I didn't know what she was doing. She came out with a yellow envelop.

"What's this?"

"I found this months ago, while I was cleaning up."

I looked at the envelop and it was opened, I don't remember this letter. It was sealed with a black kiss. I opened it and it was Jai's handwriting. This letter came all too late for me. I wish she would've been up front with me from the beginning. There's no telling how I would've reacted, but I could've saved her from herself. She took the hard route and now she was laying in the grave. I felt bad as fuck because it was my fault, even if I didn't know.

"What about it? More so why is it opened, Malia?"

"I didn't want to open it, but my mind told me to. I want to know about the girl in this letter and where is she and your child."

"Jai's dead and so is my child."

"Jai, Jai... who?"

"Jai Kendrick."

"That was Zion's sister. That's the mysterious woman." She covered her mouth as tears welled in her eyes.

"I didn't know that Jai had a brother, she never said anything about family. I found out that he was brother while in prison."

"I used to hang with her sometimes. They said that she moved away to college and I had never heard from her again."

"Yeah, she was with me for a little over two years, she had a close little relationship with her mother. I was so in love with her that it didn't bother me."

"I don't know what to say." Malia sounded stunned, I didn't blame her. It took me some time after finding out about her to wrap my head around it. I still don't want to believe it.

"Why couldn't we make our relationship work?"

"I was in a bad space Malia; some things happened and are going on that I don't have the answers to. I needed a clearer head.

"You mean with Zion, right?"

"What you mean?"

"I knew some funny shit was going on and I know how Zion works. I just didn't want to believe that he let all of that evidence come into play and pretty much lose the case. I had to work at his firm for a month and find out everything that I needed to know. I was the reason you were granted for your appeal."

"For real?"

"I believed in you Zayvier and I stand behind you. I'm glad you're home." She hugged me.

"Thank you, baby," I replied with a kiss to her lips.

"I missed you."

"You don't know how bad I missed you. I'm sorry baby, shit just looked funny as hell and I couldn't think.

"You don't have to explain. I was coming by to clean before my appointment but we took up most of the time. Would you like to go with me to the doctor?"

"Hell yeah, I want to see my baby. You don't know for sure what you're having?"

"Nope, I wanted it to be a surprise. Since you're here can we still kept the sex a secret."

"That's perfect, as long as I get to see my seed."

We made it to her appointment and the whole time I was excited. I had never been to an appointment for a pregnant woman before. Now, I was at one for my seed. I wanted to hear all the ends and outs with pregnancy; I was feeling like a schoolchild that was eager to learn.

Expected Visitors - Zion

I have been paranoid. It feels like someone is honestly watching me. It may or may not be happening, maybe everything that I've done is what has me on edge. I drowned myself in this bottle to forget my struggles and troubles. I was missing some much in my life. I fucked up a lot in my life, the one thing that I shouldn't have taken for granted is gone and I knew for sure that she wasn't coming back. Having Malia at the office a while back just let me know that she was really over me. The way that she looked and spoke to me, I can tell that it isn't laced with love anymore. But, the way she kissed me that time, I meant something; it had too. My heart hurts for her and my mind cries out for her. I want to tell her that I'm so sorry for the bullshit and really meant it this time. The first few times, I didn't mean it because I knew that I wasn't ready to give up the things that I had.

I loved Malia, but not like Malia needed to be loved. I knew that she could have done better than me on any given day, but she chose to stay with me. I wanted to love her like a husband loved his wife, but I couldn't. I knew that loving her fully could've made me a better man. I wasn't ready for that responsibility, I wasn't ready for that commitment. I fooled around on her so much that I didn't even remember what the pain felt like. I've had one or two STD's and I knew that I had them and I didn't have sex with her until I had gotten rid of them. I don't know what's wrong with me, but I can control myself with women. I hurt the ones that love me constantly.

Murdering my sister showed me what a beast that I could be. It had awakened a demon that I didn't know was there. I pierced my sister with a bullet to her brain and the moment that it happened, I felt a monster be born. I knew I was a monster because I went home and got in my bed like I didn't commit a crime. I waited for my mother to get the call that they found her body. I listened to my mother cries and went to her aid. I looked at my sister in her casket and shed tears like I wasn't the one who murdered her. I caused my family all of this grief and couldn't show an ounce of compassion for them.

I have a daughter that I hid for a year. She is my seed, my flesh and blood, someone that I must look after for the rest of her life. She was the only one that I love but I wasn't being a good father. She didn't ask to be here, but she's here now. That's one mistake that I don't regret, I just wished things went differently.

I invited Malia here to dinner tonight because I needed to speak my peace with her. I wanted to see if we could work on us. I was willing to do whatever. Looking over my appearance, I was looking damn good and I knew she couldn't resist that black on black, she loved when I dressed like this. I thought that I heard a knock on the door. I went to open and nobody was there, so I walked back to the kitchen.

"Hey baby," she greeted me. I turned around on my heels fast because I knew it couldn't be. It must be the liquor fucking me up.

"A…a…Angela!" I looked at my supposed dead baby's mother; she stood in my hallway upstairs next to Mariah's room, looking at me with those menacing eyes.

"How aren't happy to see me?" she asked with the strangest look on her face. I began walking up the stairs.

"You are supposed to be dead?"

"Am I Zion? Really am I?"

"Yes, you were in a coma."

"Yes, I was but you know what something, miraculous happened to me. I survived with no thanks to you." She pointed a gun to my head while I began walking backward down the steps. My daughter was here in the house and I needed to be careful.

"So what the hell happened?"

"I recovered."

I didn't know what else to say. I knew that this was her in a flesh, but I didn't know her. She was crazy with a stolen identity and the moment that I got near my phone, I was going to call the police. She walked me to the kitchen and I thought she didn't see my phone and I would've been able to grab it.

"Let me get this before you try to call someone." She grabbed my phone from the counter, placed in the garbage disposal, and turned it on. Now she was starting to look a little dizzy or maybe it was the alcohol. I couldn't hold my composure, I needed to sit down.

I was awakened by a slap in the face and ice-cold water being thrown on me. I thought that I was drowning. The shit got in my nose, not to mention that it was cold as fuck.

"What the fuck?" I jumped up only to be knocked back down.

"Nobody told you to get up." I looked up and saw my mother standing there.

"Mom, get this crazy bitch away from me. Go check on my daughter."

"Mariah's sleeping perfectly. But son, I want to ask you some questions." She pulled a chair and sat in front of me.

I'm sitting here drenched in a $2,000 suit and she wants to have a fucking pop quiz. Angela walk over to me with a new shirt and towel and told me to change right here in the kitchen. What the fuck is going on? Why is my dead baby momma here in my house? After I was done changing, my mother handed me an aspirin and a water. There was eerie silence that filled the room. Angela watched me as my mother watched me as well.

"I have a question, Zion," Angela broke the silence.

"What is it? When you're done I have a few of my own as well." I folded my arms across the chest.

"You never loved me, did you?" Angela began to cry. I wasn't for this shit, I was waiting on Malia to come and I wanted them gone.

"I've always told you that I wasn't in love with you. I have love for you and that's a given because you are the mother of my child."

"Children!" she screamed like a maniac. My mother and I both stared in shock at her. This bitch was really crazy.

"If it's children then where is my other child?"

"My baby died, the baby died the day that you put us into an accident"

"I'm sorry, Angela."

I felt her pain or at least I needed to act like it. I wasn't emotionally connected to the baby like that. I didn't know why I couldn't feel for a child that I supposedly help bring into the world.

"No, you're not." She slapped me and my face stung so bad. I already had a headache and this shit was blowing me for the day.

"I am. But I need to ask, if you were in a coma and survived why do I have Mariah?"

"You have Mariah because I wanted you to know what it was like being a single parent. Yeah, you used to come by every day but that's only after I had to call and harass you and your precious wife. You didn't want to do right so I had to do what I had to do."

"You could've just ask me to take her and I would've."

"You've got to be fucking kidding me, Zion. You didn't even want your wife knowing that you were a father. Your daughter, our baby, has been alive for a year now."

"I don't know how many times you want me to say the shit, Angela."

"My name isn't fucking Angela. Don't call me that bitch's name again. My name is Tasha and you know that!" she shouted, hitting herself in the head.

I looked at my mother who sat perfectly still sipping on a glass of red wine like this shit was normal. I had a dead baby mother in my living room. Why the fuck is she okay with this?

"Okay, Tasha look I'm sorry that I put you through everything that I did. I shouldn't have even taken it that far and I want you to know how truly sorry I am."

"No, you're not sorry. You left me for dead, only coming to see me one time while I was in my coma. You had your father forged my name on papers saying that I wouldn't out you as the father of my child. However, he placed hush money in my account so that I wouldn't say that you were at fault in the accident. He paid me money to go away."

I sat there with my mouth wide open. This whole time I was thinking that she was dead, but she was paid off to leave. She never explained shit to me; she just upped and left. My father was a coward, I never asked him to handle my problems for me. Yet, that was his solution.

"I never knew that. Ma, did you know?" Looking over at my mother, she still hasn't moved an ounce.

"Yes, I knew. Your father was only protecting his child."

"Protect? Yeah right."

"Your father did to you, what you couldn't do to me. Protect me."

"Protect you from what, Tasha?"

"You couldn't protect me and your children. You left us to die!" she cried out pulling out a gun, cocking the hammer, and was ready to shoot. "I hate you and I hope you rot in hell!" she screamed out as I heard a gunshot.

I closed my eyes and hoped that the Lord let me in, but I was still breathing. Opening my eyes, I saw Tasha laying in a puddle of blood. Looking behind me my mother stood there with a smoking gun in her hand. I tried to get up from the seat.

"Sit back down son," she coldly told me.

"We gotta call the police." I panicked as I watched Tasha's lifeless body as my mother stood in front of it.

"We will. Now, like I said earlier I have a question?"

"Yeah ma, what is it?"

"Why did you kill Jai?"

I felt the wind release from my soul. How did she find out? Looking at my mother, she looked numbed and tired.

"Ma, what are you talking about?" I began to get antsy in my seat. I couldn't even look her in the eyes.

"Don't play with me, Zion. Answer the question. But let me tell you this before you answer, just know that I know the truth."

"I had no choice Papa told me that I had to do it. If not, then he would kill us all. Jai was supposed to do her part and help us kill Duke. She didn't want to help her family, she couldn't be trusted, she was going to tell everything."

"So, let me get this right. You believe that your grandfather would kill his entire fucking family over some punk ass nigga."

"Yes ma, I'm so sorry."

"You took my baby girl away from me. Jai had the world at her feet. You took her away from us, me, and the world. You looked me in the eye while I had to bury my daughter. You were supposed to protect her. I don't give a fuck what your papa said; you were supposed to protect your sister."

I didn't have anything to say because she was right. I didn't protect my sister and I tore my family apart.

"I don't know what to say." I looked at the tiles on the floor when I heard a trigger being pulled.

"You're my only son that took my only daughter. I brought you in this world and now I'm going to take you out."

POW!

She sent a bullet through my chest. I couldn't move and it happened quickly.

POW!

One to the stomach, I looked at her pointing the gun at my heart.

"I love you son, but I can't allow you to breath knowing that you took a life from me. I've been dead inside since your sister's death and you knew that. Yet, you pranced around like you were just as heartbroken as I was!" she shouted and her words cut me deep.

"I love you ma and I pray that you forgive me at some point," I panted my breaths as I felt the blood seep from my mouth.

POW!

She sent one through my heart. That was it, my time was over and I couldn't blame anybody but myself. I started to feel dizzy and hot then a calm feeling came over me.

POW!

I looked at my mother as she dropped to the floor.

"I'm sorry, please forgive me," I said one last time with my final breath.

What's Understood Don't Have To Be Explained - Malia

I was so happy to have Duke home. At first, I thought that it would have been awkward but it wasn't, our chemistry still flowed. It wasn't bad being around him although I cried a time or two, I blame it on this pregnancy. We haven't gotten back together and I was okay with him. Having him back was more than enough for me. Our relationship was better than before he left. We both have grown and we both admitted to our mistakes. I missed being in his warming grace. I guess you don't know how much you miss someone until you don't have them anymore.

Speaking of people, I found out that Zion had passed away along with his mother and Tasha or Angela was what she was known by. They said that it was a murder suicide and the mother was behind it all. I couldn't believe that, I guess God places people and events in your life for a reason because that could've been me. Is it bad that I don't feel bad? I feel bad for their daughter, but that's it. She went to stay with her grandfather. Zion was a monster and I wish that he gets the rest of eternity to burn in hell.

Tonight Duke, Sasha, Dee, and I were going on a double date to dinner and a movie. I was so happy that my girl gave my bro a chance. They make each other very happy. You couldn't ask for a happier couple, well besides me and Duke when we were together. At first Duke was against it because he says that he knew how Dee was, but Dee proved us all wrong and they are going strong. Duke is constantly at my house or I was at his. He wasn't even giving me time to breathe, he said that he was making up for lost time and I was alright with that. I liked having him close and bonding.

"Come on baby, I'm hungry!" I called out to Duke while he finished getting ready.

"You're always hungry and you keep blaming that shit on my baby." He laughed while he put on his watch and helped me to the door.

"I will continue to do that until this baby is born. So, deal with it." I stuck my tongue out at him and he laughed.

The car ride to the restaurant was filled with laughter, laughter that I missed. Missing the way he starts and finishes his jokes and the way that his dimple snuck in when he smiles. I missed this man in general.

"Are you alright?" he asked as I looked out the window at the city lights.

"Yes, I'm perfect."

We arrived at the restaurant and I had seen some cheese dip on someone's plate that I wanted to order for myself. I made sure to tell Duke so that I didn't forget. My memory was terrible these days. Dee and Sasha arrived and they looked like the perfect couple, matching colors. Dee was on his grown man with the loafers, jeans, and a button up. Sasha had on a beautiful purple baby doll dress with some black laced heels. I was jealous because ever since Duke has been home, he makes me wear flats and sneakers. I know he had my best interest at heart so I don't even try to argue.

"What's up Butlers?" Dee called out as he greeted me with a hug and Duke with dap.

"Hey brother-in-law," I teased back and the look that Sasha had on her face was too cute. He showered her with a kiss. Sasha greeted us with hugs as well.

The night was chill was we clowned on each other and they mainly talked about me and my eating but I didn't care this baby had me hungry all the time. I was digging from everyone's plate. I couldn't ask for any more beautiful and wonderful people in my life.

"Baby, we gotta slow down." Duke laughed at me as he pulled the plate back from me. I gave him a look and it didn't work as he held on to the plate still.

"Baby?" Sasha asked, looking at the two of us. I shrugged my shoulders as I sipped on my virgin daiquiri.

"Yeah I said baby, sis. You gotta problem with that? She had another nigga on me while I was in the chain gang?" Duke inquired seriously. I wanted to burst out laughing because he looked like he was really mad.

"You know she wasn't about to have shit while you were locked up, bruh. I stayed on that ass. We had to make sure you got up outta there," Dee cut in and I'm glad because I wasn't about to entertain his foolishness. "We?" Duke looked at Dee and me.

"Yeah nigga we both did what we needed to do to get you home." Dee dapped him up followed with a head nod.

I looked at Duke and he had a tear in his eye. I wiped it away before placing a kiss on his lips.

"Thank y'all. Words can't express the gratitude that I have towards you two. Y'all really went all out for me to get me back home. I'm glad that I have people like y'all on my team. I have my family and yes family every one of y'all sitting here are family. But this woman right here, this is my future. Thank you." He looked around the table and lifted his glass and we followed.

"Y'all just need to get back together. Y'all are together more now than y'all were when y'all were together," Sasha chimed in and we all laughed. It really got on her nerves that we weren't together.

"You're nosy." I stuck my tongue out at her.

"What's understood don't have to be explained. This is where home is, ain't that right baby?" Duke told me and we sealed that statement with a kiss. It didn't have to said aloud to know that we were together. We understood our language of love. We had just made our relationship official with no words.

The End To A Beautiful Beginning – Duke

1 month later

When I decided to go and see about that nigga Zion, it was a long-awaited visit and I had some things I needed to handle in regards to him. I made sure that I had everything that I need to get the job down. I was going to call Dee, but this was a mission for me, Dee had nothing to do with it. Pulling up to his house, I didn't see any lights on inside only his porch light. I surveyed for a few minutes and I didn't see anyone coming or going. Walking around to the back of the house, I was able to get the lock open; it was the back door to the kitchen. Pulling out my .38 and cocking the hammer. I saw people sitting at the table. I didn't have time to think as I entered in further.

"Oh shit!"

There laid two women on the floor with bullet wounds to the head and Zion slumped over with bullet wounds to his torso. Nobody appeared to be moving; I'm sure they're dead.

"I see you fuck up somebody else's life to nigga, huh?" I looked at the three of them and I remember the older women being with Zion when Malia first called me, I think that was his mom, she had a gun in her hand. It was a fucked up picture and blood was everywhere. The other one I don't think I've ever seen her. I made sure to look around before I walked back out the door that night; I didn't leave a trace of me in that house. I guess karma paid his ass a visit, or God was looking out for me again because he knew that I was going to catch a body that night. Now that he was gone, I'm more than sure Malia was free of him for good.

My life was back intact and everything was good. I was richer and I was a completely free man. I thank my heavens every day for another chance. I'm grateful for my mistakes and my consequences. I had my woman back and my family was all good. I wanted celebrate the day, I was having my woman a party since you claimed that she couldn't do anything because she was pregnant and all. Not knowing about the party, I had to make sure that everyone kept their mouths closed. They gave into her pout more now because she was pregnant. Hell, I was the same way she had us all wrapped around her finger. This will be the first grandchild in our families. My baby was going through the motions with this pregnancy. I was cool with it right now, because I was away for majority of the pregnancy away. I'm out at stores all times a night, as well as rubbing on ass and feet at the same time.

"Baby, come on!" I called into the room as she was supposed to had been dressed by now. I had already put on her dress for her, lotioned her down so all she needed to do was tighten up her hair.

"I'm coming, baby."

I walked into the room and she looked so sexy in her beautiful laced dress. I watched her place on her earrings; the diamonds complimented her beautiful glow. I couldn't stop looking and praying over this woman. She made me a better man and she showed me what I wasn't looking for because I never knew that it existed. She tapped on my emotional surface; she made love to my mind. She held my heart and stimulated me in more than just sex.

"Surprise!" the crowd screamed out as we walked into the party.

She immediately started crying. She was shaking and all; it was so cute.

"Baby!" She slapped my arm.

She saw that it was a party but she didn't know what kind of party it was. I was nervous to the point I had to take me two shots quick as the waiter passed by.

"I did this for you because I know you haven't been feeling like yourself lately. I wanted to make you feel better and what better way than with people you love and they love you as well, right?"

"Thank you, baby. I'm so lucky to have you." She kissed my lips. Everyone walked up to us and they immediately forgot that I was standing here, they all wanted to shower her with love and affectionate, they eventually noticed me.

"I was gone say, damn just forget that I'm here," I teased them and everyone laughed. I looked at my woman as her smile was the brightest of the bunch. We walked around to greet everyone, I didn't know it was going to be this many people here. I was glad about the turn out.

Spending the night being in free spirits, I was happy as I looked around the room at family and friends. I was grateful because I wasn't supposed to be here. God blessed me and I wasn't taking another thing for granted. I may not have known that I was taking it for granted but being locked up for over a year showed me that I didn't cherish life in the manner that I really needed to. I watched my woman all night in that beautiful ass golden laced dress and the way that had her ass of hers spread and everything was looking so beautiful. The way that she carried my seed did something to my soul that I couldn't shake it. I couldn't express how I was feeling, I just know that nobody could put a hold on my soul as much as she could right now. She went through it all being with me and she's about to bless this world with my child. Damn! Fuck luck, I have the pot of gold. The way that she looked at me from across the room, I knew I needed to be by her side. She had that sexy as smirk on her face and I wanted to be under her right now.

"Hey sexy." She smiled as I grabbed her hips and hugged her tightly.

"I love you so much," I whispered with a kiss to her neck. That I love you meant so much more than what she heard.

"I love you too," she replied and that's one of the reasons she was who held the key to my heart. I could see the love in her eyes for me; through it all she's still here. Squeezing me tighter as well, feeling my words. As I continued to hug her, this energy transferred that made me grow tired, but not the tired where it's from being on the go. It was like a high, I couldn't put it into words.

They played her favorite song "Slow Jams" by Monica and Usher. I had this in the mix because this night was about her.

"My song!" she squealed as I escorted her to the dance floor. Staring into each other eyes, I spoke our language of love with a passionate kiss. I didn't care who saw us, this was my pride, joy, rib, and backbone.

Play another slow jam/ This time make it sweet/ On a slow jam/ For my baby and for me/ Play another slow jam

I watched her sing the lyrics and she couldn't sing to save her life. Yet, to me it sounded beautiful. That was the beauty of love, true love it makes you see and hear things in new lights. After the song was over we finally paid attention to our surroundings and everybody was smiling and clapping like we did a dance number. Hell, we probably did, I was so caught up that I was paying attention.

"Nigga, let me find out you've been ballroom dancing?" Dee interrupted.

"Move fool." I threw a playful punch at him and we dapped each other up.

We said our thanks on the compliments and walked to the food bar. Malia was eating up some shit and I just laughed because I knew she was going to say that it was because of the baby. Once we were done, she came and sat on my lap.

"I want you to come with me," she whispered in my ear before placing a kiss on it. She knew that shit did something to me.

"Lead the way." We left out the hotel ballroom and went to the bathroom. "Oh yeah this is how you feel?" I asked but was cut off with her kisses.

I wanted to get these dress pants down and get the dress over her head. Roaming my hands over her body, I wanted to taste her. Walking over to the door and locking it, we hungrily looked into each other's eyes. I picked her up carefully and placed her on the bathroom counter. Spreading her legs and seeing that pussy glisten with her sweet juices, I licked my lips. I was about to feed this desire for her.

"Damn," I moaned as I ran my hand over her wet clit. I can only imagine what the pussy was going feel like. I parted her clit, licked, and sucked on it. She jumped a little bit. "You aiight baby?"

Her reply was a head push back into her pussy. I felt her body relax under my touch a little more as I rubbed on her thighs. I could her panted breaths as she enjoyed this full pleasure.

"Unnh…"

I ran my hand across her beautiful baby bump as I committed my sin against her pussy. I wanted her and the pussy to both be under the spell of the lashing of my tongue. I flickered my tongue across her clit before I inserted my finger into her.

"Ooouu…" She began to vibrate and it stopped. Her pussy hugged my fingers so tightly, I had to be careful not to do too much. She moved back and forth on my fingers as I concentrated on her clit. Her juices coated my tongue and it tasted so sweet. Moaning into her pussy, it set her body under fire.

"Come on, baby!" I called out to her because the vibrating started again and I knew she was about to catch hers. Her pussy pulsated on my finger as it gripped tighter.

"Ahhhhh... fuuuuckkkkk!" she screamed at the top of her lungs. I knew that if anybody was walking by had to hear her. Hell, the people in the ballroom probably could as well. I locked my lips around her clit and tried my best to suck her dry. "Shit baby, move!" she cried out. I licked a few more times before I got up.

Looking at her face she looked drained. I looked at the mirror at myself and my beard was coated in her juices. She grabbed my shirt and kissed her scent off me, pulling down my boxers, I pulled her towards me. The moment that my dick filled that tight pussy my knees buckled. It was the first time we've had sex since God knows how long.

"Ummm..." I moaned into her neck to keep from sounding like a bitch. Her swollen pussy hugged my dick and I wanted to take my time with her. She wanted differently; she wanted the dick on some straight fucking her type shit.

"We can make love when we get home. I want you to hurt this pussy, daddy," she demanded. Her wish was my command as I as helped her off the counter and placed her feet on the floor.

She kicked her heels off and threw one leg one the counter as well. I slid in her pussy with ease as I had complete access to her walls. Gripping her hips and securing my stance in these loafers. I gave her the long strokes as she tried to throw it back on me. I wasn't about to have her doing that and hitting my seed on the counter.

"Baby, stop that shit before you hurt yourself and my kid."

"Shh... Shut the fuck up," she moaned as she continued to do what I told her not to. I pulled her back a little bit for caution without missing a beat on this pussy. I loved the sounds of her ass hitting my pelvis as it echoed off the walls. I looked at her facial expressions and the way that she bit on her bottom lip. She tried not to look at me.

"Look at ya man while he's fuckin' you right," I demanded. She was being hardheaded and she tried to keep her head up, but it kept dropping.

I wrapped my hand in her hair and pulled up. That look that she was giving me, that shit was sexy and beautiful. Giving her this dick until she felt it in her soul, I gave her a wink as she cried out. I felt something run down my leg.

"Oooouu shit, baby!" she called out.

"Why you ain't tell me you was cummin'?"

"Shiiiit baby!"

This shit wasn't like her normal nut. This shit was making a puddle on the floor.

"Fuck!" I pulled out of her. "I think your water broke."

She looked down and noticed that in fact her water was broken.

"Oh my god!" She started to panic.

"Not now baby." I tried to calm her down as I tried to wipe her up, but the shit was still coming out.

"What the hell you mean not now, Duke? My water broke while I was catching a nut."

I wanted to hold in my laughter but she was so serious. She's pissed about how her water broke, she should be happy that the baby is coming instead.

"I think that you owe me a thank you." I wiped her up and pulled her dress down. There wasn't too damage to her dress, but my pants had wet stains all the way down to the shoes. Going back into the ballroom, I said, "Aye, we gotta go y'all, Malia's in labor!"

My momma, sisters, Sasha, and even Dee was frantic. I needed them to get us to the hospital and in one piece. They helped her to the car, while I told the hotel staff on the way out the door that the party was over. Malia was in the car trying to keep her cool, but her thoughts were running.

"I can't have my baby in this truck. Dee, bro, please get me to the hospital"

"Baby he will. We're fifteen minutes away but he's going to get you there."

"Noooo!" she cried out as she screamed again.

"What's wrong?"

"Contractions." She practiced her breathing. "Time them, they're coming too fast."

Now I was about to panic. "Dee, nigga push this shit. If you get a ticket, I got you."

I heard the engine on this Denali roar and I knew he was about to drift this shit. I trusted him and I couldn't think about that, I just wanted my woman and child to be healthy and safe. Malia's contractions were coming every three minutes. We pulled up to hospital and I barely let the truck stop before I was out.

"My wife is about to give birth in the back of my truck!" I screamed out to nobody, just whoever could get her some help. Doctors and nurses ran past me with a wheelchair. My mother and everybody else came into the hospital. They had to sit in the waiting room. The moment that they got her to her room, she was ready to go.

"I can't have this baby right now. The baby is a few weeks early."

"It's perfectly okay Malia you're thirty-six weeks, that's perfect," the doctor told her as he instructed the nurses on what to do. They were setting up fast as hell and I hoped that they had everything that they needed.

"Okay doc. Can I get an epidural?"

The doctor checked her cervix.

"I'm sorry Malia, but the baby is ready. Your past your ten centimeters, it's time to work."

"Wait, what? No! I need drugs!" she cried out because another contraction hit.

"It's gone be okay, baby. Let's get the baby here." I kissed her.

"Malia, I need you to push on your next contraction."

I watched her give her all, the hard work that it was taking her and the strength that it took her to have a baby naturally. I knew now was the time, it may sound crazy but it felt right.

"Arghhhh!! Please!" she screamed out.

"Malia?"

"What the fuck you want, Duke?" She turned into a beast with sweat dripping from her head. I opened the box and her eyes got big.

"1.2.3. push, Malia" the doctor coached again.

"Get this baby up outta me."

"Will you marry me?" I asked as she squeezed my hand.

"Yes, I'll marry you baby. But now isn't the time... we're kind of in the middle of something." She pushed again.

My hand was swollen as hell and I just knew that she had broken my shit. Once she laid back down, I heard my baby's cry. I walked around to see my beautiful baby girl. I began to cry as the doctor handed me the scissors to cut the umbilical cord before placing her in my arms. My baby girl was so beautiful with a head full of thick curly hair, with all fingers and toes. She had her mother's nose, but she was my twin. I placed my daughter in her mother's arms.

"Heavenly Father;

Thank you for this beautiful blessing, my daughter and now my wife. You've truly outdone yourself and I thank you for seeing me through so that I could be here to witness it. Thanking you in advance for the blessings that are to come. I'm forever in your mercy.

In your name... I pray... Amen."

I placed a kiss on them both.

"You look beautiful baby and thank you for giving it all to me," I told her while placing the ring on her finger.

"This was meant to be and thank you for loving me and giving me this beautiful blessing, Miss Bella London Butler."

"Bella, I love that name," I replied, looking at my sleeping daughter.

"That was beautiful," the doctor said as the nurses clapped. "Congratulations on your new princess and your upcoming nuptials."

We had to let them clean her up and take her to the nursery. I was there every step of the way too, I needed to see that they were treating my daughter right. When they were done with her, I went to the waiting room to let everyone know that she was here. They were excited about it being a girl and they couldn't wait to see her.

"My grandbaby," my mother cooed, taking her from my arms. My mother had gotten her wish of a grandchild.

"Bitch!"

"Shh… damn Sasha, you gone wake my baby up." I laughed at her loud ass.

"I'm sorry but something happened while we were in the waiting room because Malia didn't have on this ring." Everyone looked at her finger.

"I'm getting married!!"

"You broke code, nigga." Dee chimed in.

"How?"

"You had us throw the party so you could propose and then you make her go into labor trying to blow her back out. Then you propose anyway."

Everyone laughed at Dee; he was a fool, but there was truth to all his statements.

"Things don't always go according to plans, my boy."

Malia was tired and I decided to stay up for Bella. The whole night I stayed up watching them both sleep. I couldn't believe that we made something so wonderful. That was our lovechild and I wouldn't change a thing, this was my blessing. I thank my heavenly father on the regular because he didn't have to see me through. He did and he showed me that all things were greater through him, especially when you believe. I was the boss in the streets at one point, but I met an even greater boss that I didn't mind bowing down to, Malia and now our daughter Bella, they had both captured my heart.

THE END!

Thank you,

Social Media Contacts:

Instagram

@justcallmemyia

Twitter

@MYiA_DUhH

Facebook Page

Myia White

Facebook Like Page

https://www.facebook.com/AuthorMyia/#

Amazon's Author Page

amazon.com/author/myiawhite

CPSIA information can be obtained
at www.ICGtesting.com
Printed in the USA
LVOW11s2301060417

529953LV00001B/88/P